THE FLYING RED HORSE
by Frances Crane

The only problem Jean Abbott anticipated as she drove to Dallas to meet her detective husband Patrick. was what to do with their dachshund Pancho. They left him with Sally, the daughter of Iles Dollahan, a wealthy oil man, and that night Pancho discovered the body of Juliana Willoz, Mrs. Dollahan's younger sister, on the Dollahan lawn.

But who would kill Juliana, the docile, unambitious, dowdy Juliana—especially when it was the youngest sister, Rosemary Willoz, who fished for trouble?

The interference with the Abbotts' detecting is a little rough in Dallas, for despite their lavish wealth the Dollahans came up the hard way, and they all know how to handle a gun. The contrast between the nice manners of new money and the old direct-action methods of the oil fields provides grim comedy as the Abbotts, working on their own, outface the Dollahans and outguess the police—but just barely.

This is another top-flight example of Frances Crane's mastery of the suspense-till-the-end novel of murder. Others have been *Black Cypress, the Cinnamon Murder, The Indigo Necklace,* etc.

THE FLYING RED HORSE

Other books by Frances Crane

MURDER ON THE PURPLE WATER

THE AMETHYST SPECTACLES

THE PINK UMBRELLA

THE YELLOW VIOLET

THE GOLDEN BOX

THE APPLEGREEN CAT

THE TURQUOISE SHOP

THE INDIGO NECKLACE

THE SHOCKING PINK HAT

THE CINNAMON MURDER

BLACK CYPRESS

THE FLYING RED HORSE

BY FRANCES CRANE

Original printing, 1949
All Rights Reserved

For
BENNETT CERF

1

DUSK was closing in as we rolled along Route 77 and, across the green alfalfa fields, saw the lights pricking out in the piled-up skyscrapers of Dallas, Texas. Light fountained above one and on top of another was a great flying red horse, which turned slowly like a weathervane in a soft but steady wind. Definitely the scene was strictly modern, but for the moment it seemed as improbable as a picture in a fairy tale.

"We should be knights in armor, Pancho. Galloping towards that sparkling city across this blue-green plain."

My companion, a satiny brown dachshund, sniffed rapturously at the alfalfa and wagged his skinny little tail.

My husband, and Pancho's master, Patrick Abbott, would not be as happy to see Pancho as Pancho would be to see him. But, darling, I would say, he wanted so much to come. After all, six hundred miles is a long way to drive entirely alone. But how many times, dear, Patrick would answer, must I ask you not to bring the dog when we're stopping at a hotel? Hotels and dogs don't mix, Patrick would say, and I would say, smiling,

"But this is Texas. Everybody in Texas is so broad-minded that of course the hotel will take in our dog."

And Pancho would listen, his ears up, his big eyes so full of loving kindness that Patrick would break down.

"How a dog his size can be such a regular dog beats me, Jean."

"It's the life-sized dachshund character, Pat."

"Nuts. He's merely cockeyed. He's little and he can't bring himself to admit it."

"He knows everything, Pat. Strictly everything."

"Too bad he can't talk."

Using the flying red horse as a guide I drove towards the skyscrapers and after a few minutes arrived outside the Hotel Adolphus. Here we were to meet Patrick Abbott.

A doorman opened the car door and took my keys. He made no objection to Pancho. A colored boy sallied forth to collect my bags. He said I sure had a mighty pretty little dog. So far, swell, I thought. I snapped the leash onto Pancho's collar and we stepped out on the sidewalk.

"Oh, Kim! Look! Isn't he a dream? He's the very picture of Sam."

What a lovely voice, I thought.

"He sure is, Sally," a boyish voice replied to the lovely girlish voice.

"Oh, Kim! Sam really was murdered. I had a post mortem."

"Darling," Kim said.

This startling piece of conversation demanded attention.

I looked at them and met the starry-eyed glance of a tall, slim girl with a small face, thick brown hair, green eyes, a small straight nose, and a sweet wide mouth. She wore a gray flannel suit and on the crown of her head a small gray felt cloche. With her was a taller boy, also dressed in gray, with broad shoulders, gray eyes, a very dark sun-tan, and a sunburned crew cut. They were in love and didn't care who knew it. So I smiled at them. They smiled back.

Then I followed Pancho into the hotel. As usual, he knew exactly what to do.

Patrick was in the lobby. Tall and lean, with long blue eyes, very dark hair, his slender western face extra brown from two weeks of South Texas sunshine, he was standing just beyond the top of the worn marble steps which led up from the main entrance of the hotel. With him was a big broad-shouldered, blue-eyed gray-haired man and a slim, stylish woman who looked like a chic witch.

Patrick spied me at once and I saw the love light come into his eyes, even though they also spied Pancho. He hurried to meet me and kissed me, hard.

He stooped to pat Pancho, who was about to wag himself into two parts.

"How come the dog, Jeanie?"

"Well, he wanted so to come, and . . ."

"Nuts," Patrick said fondly. He kissed me again. "I doubt if the hotel will take him. We'll find out later. Come along and meet the Dollahans. Iles Dollahan was one of the oil men I met while on this Houston case we've just finished. Amanda is his second wife."

Introductions were made. Iles had a deep voice and warm manner which made you sense his real friendliness. Amanda was gray-haired but a lot younger than her husband. Twenty years, I guessed, or even more. Her bewitching face was heart-shaped. Her eyes were a deep velvety black. Her skin was ivory and her only make-up was her ruby-red lipstick. Her smile was formal but not uncordial. She wore black, carried a big armful of minks, wore some stunning ruby earrings in the pointed lobes of her ears, and clipped at her throat were two ruby-packed replicas of the horse which flies over Dallas.

Probably thinking of her very superior nylons, Amanda moved away slightly when she looked at Pancho.

"Cute little dog," Iles said. "What's his name?"

"Pancho," I said.

"Pancho?" Amanda asked. "What a queer name for a dachshund."

"Not for him, Mrs. Dollahan. Pancho comes from a fine old Spanish dachshund family."[1]

"Spanish? How quaint!"

"The little fellow looks like Sam, Amanda," Iles Dollahan said.

"I daresay he does. They all look alike, Iles, dear."

The lady is cultivated as hell, I thought. She chooses every word in advance and spits it out whole.

"Iles?" called a sweet voice. It was the girl in gray. She came flying up the steps, followed by the boy with the sunburned crew cut.

---

[1] *The Yellow Violet.*

"Honey!" Iles said. He kissed her and nodded at the boy. "Like you to meet my daughter Sally, Mrs. Abbott."

"Hello," we said.

"And Kim Forsythe. Kim's one of our engineers. He and Pat are acquainted already."

"What fun!" Sally Dollahan said. "We saw you outside, remember? We were talking about your dog. Isn't he beautiful, Iles? He looks exactly like Sam." To me, "Sam was my dachshund."

Amanda said in her precise, toneless voice, "We hope you will dine with us tonight, Mrs. Abbott." I glanced at Patrick. His eyes said to accept. I said thank you and Amanda said, "Around eightish, at the Club. I'm sorry we can't have you at the house. It's the servants' night out, you see."

"We've told Pat how to get to the Club," Iles said. I had misgivings now, for I had not come prepared to dine with anybody quite as elegant as Amanda.

"Must we dress, Mrs. Dollahan? If so. . . ."

"Hell, no," Iles said. "Come the way you are."

"Formal clothes are not necessary," Amanda said, in the kind of tone that makes you think like fish they're not. "I'm afraid you'll have to do something about your dog, though. This hotel does not allow dogs, and the Club . . ."

"Oh, damn the Club," Iles said. "Bring the little fellow right along."

"Let me keep him," Sally Dollahan said. She was so earnest about it I felt a little puzzled. "He'll be all right with me. I'd just love to have him all the time you're here."

"Sure she would," her father said. "Sally is just crazy about dachshunds. Don't you worry about that little dog, Mrs. Abbott, so long as he's with Sally."

I now looked at Pancho, since he was the one to decide this, really. He was sitting up on his small haunches and looking up at Sally and wagging his little front feet. He looked like a brown penguin. That our dog should fall so hard and so serenely for somebody he had only just met gave a kind of pang. But anyhow that settled the problem of

Pancho at the moment—and also led to complications that no one could have foreseen.

We had a suite on one of the top floors. Through the slanted louvers I could see that great flying red horse, still high above us.

I took a good look at the horse after Patrick stopped kissing me, and I said, "Did you notice those ruby clips Amanda Dollahan was wearing, Pat? I suppose they were rubies."

"They are," Patrick said.

"Oh. You know?"

"I wasn't told it, but they would be."

"You mean, they've got money?"

"Who hasn't in Dallas? Gee, you're sweet, Jeanie. Why talk about money? I wish we didn't have to go out to dinner. We could call room service, order up dinner with champagne, shut out the world, and. . . ."

"Hey? I've been in seclusion while you've been away. Up in Northern New Mexico, remember? We're heading back to New Mexico in a couple of days and you can shut the world out up there."

Patrick groaned.

"Anyhow we have to go. It's business, in a way. Iles didn't tell me exactly what's on his mind but he said in Houston that he had something he wanted to consult me about. We flew up this afternoon in his private plane. His pilot was with us, and also Kim Forsythe, so Iles didn't open up about whatever it is he's worrying about. I'm to see him about that in the morning. What was your impression of the Dollahans, Jean?"

"First, a cigarette."

"Okay." Patrick gave me one and took one himself. "Sit on my lap while we smoke these."

He gave me a light and chose the best chair and cradled me, after long experience, expertly.

"Iles, I go for," I said. "Also his lovely daughter Sally. Also her boyfriend, Kim. They make a beautiful pair. Amanda . . . well, I don't know."

"She's very brainy, Iles says."

"I'm sure of it. Somehow I don't vibrate to Amanda. Maybe it's because she seems too perfect."

"Amanda is one of the Willoz sisters."

"Who?"

"Dallas girls. I heard about them in Houston, but not from Iles. Like Iles Dollahan, the sisters started from scratch. There are three of them. Amanda is the eldest. Juliana is a year younger than Amanda. Juliana was divorced from Ulysses B. Green, said to be one of the richest men in the oil business. The third is Rosemary, who is much younger than the other two. She married some elderly gent or other when she was sixteen and the marriage was annulled. Juliana calls herself *Mrs.* Willoz. Rosemary is *Miss* Willoz. Rosemary lives with the Dollahans."

"Why all this detail?"

"You'll meet them at dinner. Thought you might like to get the dope on them first. I have a hunch that what Iles wants to talk to me about is a family affair. I'd like you to keep your eyes open. From what I've heard, Amanda Dollahan is the smart one of the three sisters. Juliana doesn't seem to register specially. Rosemary is said to be pretty as a peach. She's about Sally's age, I should guess. Iles struck it very rich about six years ago. Amanda was then his secretary. She is credited with much of his financial success. Iles is a wonderful guy, Jean. No education to speak of, climbed the ladder all by himself."

"And there sat Amanda. At the top, in her web."

"Hey?"

I put his hand against my face.

"I'm jealous. I'm jealous of her chic. I'm jealous of her flying ruby horses, specially. They're the smartest gadgets I've seen."

Patrick said, "Would you like something like them, set with emeralds?"

"*Pat!*"

"But you don't need to hanker after anybody's gadgets, Jean. I love buying emeralds, but every time I've wanted to, since we got married . . ."

"Idiot! Steak is a dollar and a quarter a pound. Mike's nurse costs a mint. We haven't yet paid off the mortgage on our house in San Francisco. We can't bring ourselves to give up my old adobe cottage in New Mexico. What I mean is that the things we insist on doing and having, which cost more than we can afford, absolutely prohibit buying stuff like emeralds."

"I ought to be in the oil business," Patrick said.

"Don't be silly, darling. Who wants rubies and emeralds? Only the people who have nothing better. And we do."

"Darling," Patrick said.

"Go on. Tell me more about the Dollahans."

"There isn't any more, yet. Sally and Kim Forsythe are engaged but that seems to be very okay with Iles, so my hunch is that whatever's worrying him has to do either with Amanda or one of her sisters."

2

FORTUNATELY, even though I do not own fine and numerous minks, San Francisco clothes need not do any second-fiddling even to those of Dallas, Texas. I had not brought evening clothes, but I had a new dinner outfit in a rich black, a creation with a snug, short jacket and a grand long-enough skirt. The blouse—what there was of it—was a print of pure silk, not a banal print, but one in which a very keen emerald vied with touches of black and shocking pink, very nice, and for Mrs. Patrick Abbott, very expensive. My hat was a Sally Victor spot which looked especially designed for the suit.

Examining myself critically, before emerging into the snappy city of the flying red horse, I decided that I could pass muster. My emerald earrings were modest, but genuine. My emerald engagement ring was not gaudy, but experts had commended its quality. My emerald bracelet, ditto.

"I don't know how you do it, baby," Patrick said.

"Do what?"

"Not a line around the amber eyes. Not a gray hair in the black, black wig."

"Your eyesight isn't what it used to be, dear."

"Maybe it's my dotage."

Patrick kissed me. "I'm all fixed for the party. If you don't stop manhandling me, my own dotage will set in, Pat."

"Damn the party!"

We were ten minutes late. At their Club Iles and Amanda Dollahan and Rosemary Willoz were waiting in a smartly-styled lounge. There was a deep pile carpet and a dashing fabric in the slip-covers. An artistic bouquet adorned an artistic niche. Music played somewhere. Adjacent to the lounge was a softly lighted bar and beyond it a circular dining room.

Iles suggested a drink while we waited for the remaining dinner guests and, in the bar, we gathered around a table large enough for eight.

Psychologists, no doubt, go in huddles with themselves over the drinks their specimens choose. An expert in character analysis could tell you why Amanda had a martini, Iles straight rye, with a water chaser, Patrick a scotch and soda, and even why I had a dry bourbon Manhattan.

Rosemary Willoz chose a Cloverleaf cocktail. I decided it was because the pink color of the drink matched Rosemary. She was all pink and white, small, fragile-looking and blonde. You looked at Rosemary and she looked like a pure young girl. You had a second glance and she was smiling a pink crescent-shaped smile and she looked like a harlot. She wore a fluffy white dress with a pink ribbon sash, and a string of small pearls. Crowning her long pale hair was a wreath of pale pink camellias.

She is a type you need to keep an eye on, I thought. If only because she looks good enough to eat. Men find those clean, pink, edible-looking gals, irresistible.

Amanda Dollahan wore an oyster-white dinner dress, with a low, square neckline caught at the corners with her flying ruby horses. She wore rubies in flower-shaped earrings and in two handsome bracelets. Her engagement ring was a large blood red ruby, and her wedding ring was encircled with these stones in the same fine, deep shade. Obviously Amanda loved rubies. Also they loved Amanda. They suited her perfectly.

Iles had changed to a dark lounge suit. He seemed now in the prime of life, dignified, handsome, bronzed, with shining blue eyes under his straight heavy eyebrows, and the quick generous smile of a man you would instantly trust. He was in a fine mood.

He said, "Sally isn't coming tonight."

I felt disappointed. Iles's daughter attracted me in the same way as himself.

"I hope it isn't our dog?"

"Not at all. She could have fetched him here and we'd've parked him at the desk. No, it was something else. She's still upset about her own dog Sam, too. I told her tonight she'd got to get herself another dachshund and stop this grieving."

Rosemary had a little girl's voice.

"I just can't understand anybody's being so crazy over animals as Sally. Though of course Sam was different. Sam really was a sweet dog."

"Sam was killed by a motorcar," Amanda said. "He ventured across the creek at the edge of our lawn and got run down on the boulevard. We think he tried to get home afterward and drowned in the creek."

(Sam was murdered, Sally had said to Kim Forsythe, there outside our hotel. She had had a post-mortem, she said.)

"Sam was cute. But *so* nosey," Rosemary said.

Patrick grinned at her, in his eyes the half-tender, half-mischievous expression which all men use when talking to all girls like Rosemary.

"That's the breed, Miss Willoz. Dachshunds think they have to pry into other people's business."

"Sure enough?" Rosemary inquired, trustingly.

For goodness' sake, I thought. Girls like her went out before World War One.

"They say that breed wasn't much good in the Army," Iles said.

"Do too much original thinking," Patrick said.

"Wouldn't be surprised," Iles chuckled in reply. They grinned at each other. Patrick likes Iles a lot, I thought. They were probably pretty much the same kind. Easy on the surface. Deep as a well inside.

Rosemary had contrived to sit beside Patrick. She watched him with her oval face tilted, her blue eyes trusting, her pink lips curved in her pussycat smile.

Her smile is older than Egypt, I thought. And it always works. Men always fall for it. Gosh.

"I've heard so much about you, Mr. Abbott."

"I hope you've heard good, Miss Willoz."

"First names, please," Iles said. "We're going to see a lot of you folks, I hope. Might as well start out friendly."

"Rather," Amanda said, perfunctorily.

"You're so good-looking, Pat," Rosemary said. "I always heard that detectives were fat or bald or something and wore wrinkled old clothes so that people wouldn't look at them twice. I reckon I must have been mistaken . . . Pat."

"Definitely, Rosemary."

"Sure enough?"

"Sure enough. We're all handsome, Rosemary. We never carry guns and if we should happen to have one on, accidentally, we always refrain from shooting women in the back. We never kick even a man when he is down. We shoot a cardsharp on sight, if we happen to have the gun, and we never drink whisky or kiss the other fellow's girl."

Amanda smiled her precise smile and Rosemary's laughter tinkled like a silver bell. Her forget-me-not blue eyes looked into Patrick's with childlike innocence, but her medieval smile told him he might change his mind when it came to kissing other girls.

Can this girl be? I asked myself. Very definitely she could. There she sat, with Patrick falling for her, and Amanda gazing fondly at her, and me having to pretend I liked it.

Fondness and love came into Amanda's face whenever she looked at Rosemary.

"Would you take Rosemary and me for sisters, Jean?" The first name did not come as easy to Amanda as to Iles. "Juliana and I look alike. We look like our father. Rosemary is like Mother. She came along when Julie and I were already big girls, and when our parents died Rosemary was only ten, so she really was our baby."

"Three sisters with no brothers are always dramatic," I said. That didn't sound right from me, either. Amanda and Rosemary exchanged glances.

And then Juliana Willoz arrived, announcing ahead of her that Lucius and Kim would be right in.

Her resemblance to Amanda was superficial. She was rather like a caricature of her stylish older sister, for she was carelessly dressed in a black dress, with a mangy-looking wrap of some dark shiny fur. Her hair was dyed auburn. Her black eyes were beady, her nose too big, and her chin too long, and you learned pronto that she was a bore.

Lucius Brady seemed to be a friend of the family. He kissed Amanda, shook hands with Iles, flapped a gay hand at Rosemary, and acknowledged us with ceremony. Another medieval item, I thought.

"Lemonade, Julie?" Iles asked.

Juliana smiled gaily, showing nice teeth.

"Not tonight, Iles. Champagne cocktail, tonight."

"What?" Amanda asked. She smiled at us. "Juliana is our teetotaler."

"Not tonight, but don't ask why," Juliana said, coquettishly.

"And for you, Brady?"

There was a change in Iles's tone, a coolness, when he addressed Brady.

"My usual, Iles. Dry martini, with an onion." Brady's voice made your spine feel like a harp string.

He was anything but handsome, and in his late forties at least, and only medium tall. His hair was graying, his face horsey. His blue eyes had a dreamy look which Patrick declared was due to his being nearsighted. He had a wide, heavy mouth, but his smile was beautiful because he had beautiful teeth.

The drinks were brought. Juliana lifted her glass. "Tomorrow I'll tell you my secret."

"Well, here's to whatever it is, Julie," Iles said comfortably.

"Must be exciting," Amanda said, a trifle tartly.

Brady said, "Isn't she tantalizing, Amanda?. Driving me here from my hotel she talked this same way. We've got to find out what she's up to."

"We'll find out," Amanda said indifferently. "How long will you be in Dallas this time, Lucius?"

"Depends. I planned to fly back to New York tomorrow, but something has come up."

Amanda's velvety eyes watched him. Juliana darted him an excited glance. Rosemary gave him a long sky-blue look and smiled her hypnotic smile. There was no further interest in Juliana's exciting secret. She didn't expect it.

She is the kind sister, the vulgar one, the dull one, I thought, and turned my attention to Kim Forsythe.

He was grim. He had downed a double bourbon straight and was already having another. I contrasted him to the way I had seen him outside our hotel when I had arrived in Dallas. Then he was frank and boyish, carefree, happy, his gray eyes shining with love for Sally Dollahan. They were a pair.

Now Sally was absent and Kim was sunk and would rather be absent, too, if his present behavior meant anything. I felt sorry, the way you always do when things are not clicking as they should between a couple of very nice kids.

The talk had moved into local affairs. There was chatter about things and people unfamiliar to me, about Theatre '48, Hockaday School, Brookhollow, the Dallas Country Club, the Cipango Club. From there it went to personalities. It was interesting to hear how Amanda Dollahan and Lucius Brady, working as a team, kept any open hint of malice out of gossip which was, I imagined, definitely malicious.

We went on from the cocktail room to dinner. The Club was locally famous for its Creole cuisine. There was good reason.

Later on, we went as Lucius Brady's guests to the Mural Room in the Baker Hotel, where we were to catch the supper show.

Rosemary Willoz contrived to ride from the Club to the hotel with Patrick. I rode in a handsome Cadillac town car with Amanda and Kim Forsythe and Iles, who did the driving. Brady rode again with Juliana Willoz. In the Mural Room later I said, "I'm surprised you asked me for the first dance, Patrick, de-ar."

"I'd get hell if I didn't, sugar-pie."

"Did you learn that Texas sweet-talk from Rosemary, lamb?"

"What do you think, lamb-pie?"

"Well, if you did, I hope she fades young or something."

"Tut," Patrick said. "Tut, ma'am."

"Seriously, she's a smart cooky, I bet. But you're wasting good time. She's after Lucius Brady."

"Mustn't let it happen, ma'am. That roué? Over my dead body, s' help me."

"I'm being serious and you would do well to listen, Patrick Abbott. The competition between the Willoz sisters for that aging item from New York is intense. Mark my word, and never say I didn't warn you."

Rosemary came by just then, dancing with Kim Forsythe, her face planked somewhere just above his stomach, her little smile against his nice dark jacket. He looked mad enough to crack a couple of her tough little vertebrae. He hadn't said a word all evening. Now he was talking a streak. I called Patrick's attention to Kim's golden opportunity to do Rosemary in. He declared that the only person present in imminent danger was Juliana Willoz. If she didn't stop talking, Patrick said, somebody would resort to an axe. This concluded our ill-bred remarks about our hosts at that time.

3

LUCIUS BRADY was the country girl's—which means me—notion of a sophisticated New Yorker. He was always at ease, yet he never gave the impression of being easily approachable. He spoke with a smart accent, clipped and sure, but never stiff or exaggerated. You imagined he would feel at home in any city, but never in the country, and that he could take on the color of whatever city he was in with a chameleon's celerity. Dallas would be home to him as easily as Paris, but when in Dallas never by word or sign would he suggest that New York or Paris or London or Rome or any other old and celebrated place might be even a trifle superior.

His party this evening was expensive and unostentatious. It was in perfect taste. We ate simple, costly things. The champagne was the best. It flowed freely and of itself would have made the supper party memorable. Brady behaved as though he were entertaining in his private home. The waiters, no doubt very well tipped and probably accustomed to his ways, seemed to take a special interest in looking after his guests. He was on terms of chatty acquaintance with the orchestra leader and the entertainers. And there was never a slow moment, nor an uncouth one, and we all felt sorry when the hour arrived when the restaurant had legally to close.

By now the edges of my first impressions had worn off, possibly because of the champagne, and I felt kindly towards everyone, even Rosemary. But Juliana was very tiresome. She was so ceaselessly glad.

Kim was staying, like ourselves, at the Adolphus. As we crossed the lobby of the Baker Hotel on leaving the Mural Room Iles said, "Now you must come and see our house, folks. It was really what I wanted you to do most, but I had forgotten that this is the night our help takes off. All of you come. Kim, you come too. You can ride back down town with the Abbotts, maybe."

"And I'll fetch Lucius!" Juliana said, gladly.

Iles's face showed plainly that he didn't want Brady. But to omit him would be rudeness, after his charming party, and Amanda hastened to insist.

I managed to ride back with Patrick.

"Rosemary is nothing but a type, Pat," I conceded generously.

"That does for her," Patrick said.

"Seriously. And she collects. She collects men. She hates to see any get away. Once you admit that, she's just silly."

"Unless it's *your* man."

"Naturally. I wonder what Kim was saying to her? Something tough, I think. I'm glad Kim's going back to the house. Iles wanted him to come because of Sally."

"Could be."

"Rosemary's very keen about Brady. Probably because he's difficult to collect. They're all after him, hard."

"Do you infer that Amanda would stoop to an impurity?"

"Certainly not. Perhaps Lucius Brady impresses her and she merely wants to impress him back."

"Brady would be a hard guy to impress, Jean. Hard to impress. Hard to collect. That does for Brady."

"What does he do?"

"He sells jewels. In a big way. The crazier women are about Brady the easier his job is probably. He's with Ferrier's, the big jewelry house in New York. He just fetched Amanda those ruby clips. Executing her special order, he called it—it was her idea but Ferrier's design. They are very beautiful stuff. They set Iles Dollahan back a fat hunk of oil money. Now you know all I know, so we'll never mention Brady again."

"How much do you suppose the red horses cost?"

"Iles said fifteen thousand for the pair. They were cheap at the price. Many of the rubies are of good size and all are the very best color. They are Burma rubies, the pigeon-blood red kind which is so highly prized."

"For goodness' sake. How did you learn all that?"

"From Amanda, dear. What do you think Amanda and I talked about while we were dancing? Her flying red horses, of course. They're her passion."

"They and Rosemary and Lucius Brady. . . . Isn't this the way we took when we came out to their Club?"

"Yes. Their house is a little beyond the Club. On the opposite bank of Turtle Creek."

The night was warm and the moon was shining. There was the satiny feeling of sin in the air, but as far as I could make out from the car, the sky was cloudless. The air was heavy with an indefinable aromatic sweetness, the smell of early spring. The trees were in bud. Daffodils and hyacinths and forsythia bloomed along the way.

"We mustn't stay long, Pat. Amanda doesn't really want us. And you have to get up early. Didn't I hear you make a date with Iles for seven in the morning?"

"Yep. He's having breakfast with me before flying out to Odessa. Kim is going with him. They've got trouble of some kind out on a lease. Sounds rugged. I heard Iles ask Kim if he remembered to fetch his gun."

"Just like Texas in the movies. It was nice of you to dance with Juliana, Pat."

"I'm a very nice guy, Jean. Because Juliana can't dance. Also she talks all the time. Amanda is an adequate dancer and Rosemary is a cuddly little armful of sweet-scented fluff, but Juliana. . . . And do you appreciate the fact that I danced not once, but twice, with Juliana?"

"That was sweet. Really it was, dear."

"I say. And she told me her secret."

"She did?"

"I'm not allowed to tell you, Jeanie."

"That's all right. I can wait. The awful thing about the secrets of girls like Juliana is that you can wait to know them."

"Juliana has a better time than either of the others," Patrick said. "She doesn't know she's a dud. She's happy about every little thing. She is satisfied with life just as it comes. She had always been taken advantage of, but she is incapable of resentment. She is entirely unselfish. I guess nothing is as boring as complete unselfishness."

"Unless it's complete gladness. Well, that settles Juliana. I hope our Pancho is behaving himself."

"By this time that conceited canine will have taken over the premises."

Iles drove ahead of us. Juliana's car, with Brady at the wheel, followed us at about half a block. We drove under a trestle or a viaduct, and on our right I saw Turtle Creek. It wasn't a large stream, and obviously it was flooded. In the moonlight you could see the water moving at a fast pace. The creek was thickly edged with trees and shrubs not yet in leaf. You saw the water through a lacework of twigs and branches.

We were stopped by a red light. Ahead of us Iles slowed down, and when we could move on circled with his left hand to indicate that we were to make the next turning to the right.

He turned, turned back immediately along the opposite bank of the creek, crossed a bridge and followed a narrow one-way street. The water was close beside us for a short distance. Then the street angled away and there were houses between us and the creek. Iles turned into a graveled drive and went on into a large garage. There was wide parking space outside. We parked here and Brady parked over to our right. Either car had room to go out without the other having to be moved.

In the stillness which followed the hush of the three motors the night was full of the sound of rushing water and the trilling of countless frogs. The air was rich with the scent of the hyacinths which bordered the curving flagstone walk from the parking space to the main entrance of the house.

The Dollahan house was painted white, two stories high, and built with a central portion and two wings. The servants' quarters were over the garage, which was separated by a covered terrace angling from the kitchen wing of the house.

Inside, the house was in the American colonial tradition, with a central hall from the main entrance to a terrace which ran the full length of the house along the creek. There were deep pile carpets, pale walls, white wood-work, mahogany furniture of classic design, pictures in heavy gold-leaf frames, and upholstery in pale colors. The house lacked color, but it made a fine neutral background for the deep reds and rich blues which I later learned that Amanda loved to wear. The place lacked personality, except Sally's room and Iles Dollahan's bar.

Patrick and Kim and Lucius Brady went off at once with Iles to the pine-paneled room he called the bar.

Amanda was showing me the dining room when there was a rush on the stairs and Pancho came down, followed by Sally Dollahan. She had changed to a white off-the-shoulder blouse and a long full skirt and ballet slippers. Her wonderful hair was shining, and hanging free in a long page-boy style.

Rosemary and Juliana had vanished into the downstairs powder room. Amanda, on seeing Pancho, hastily joined them.

"How has Pancho behaved, Sally?"

"He's wonderful. He spent the evening guarding me the way a good dog always does."

I laughed. "Pat said he would have taken over the premises, Sally. We missed you this evening."

"I . . . I didn't want to come. Will you lunch with me tomorrow?"

"I'd love to. I'm shopping in the morning."

"Then how about lunching at Neiman's? Say about one."

"It's a date," I said. Sally suddenly froze. I said, "What's wrong?"

I needn't've asked because Kim was coming into the hall from the living room.

"Sally, if you will only let me explain?" he said.

"I'm sorry."

Kim looked the picture of misery. His mouth trembled. His gray eyes were dark with anguish.

Sally lifted a honey-colored shoulder.

"Jean, will you come see my room?"

Kim's lips hardened. Without another word he left the house. He went out by way of the terrace. I saw the gleam of the water in the creek before the door closed.

Now Sally's lips were trembling. Her eyes filled with tears.

I went with her upstairs. Pancho showed us the way quite as if he had always lived here. In her room which overlooked the creek he at once went to a basket which had belonged, Sally said, to Sam. The room was done in modern style with a good deal of white and some yellow. It was attractive, informal, and young.

"Amanda had it antique," Sally said. "But I wanted it this way and Iles said to do what I liked. I had most of these things in college."

"Where did you go, Sally?"

"Austin," Sally said. I remembered that the State University is at Austin. "Smoke?"

"Thanks."

We settled down for a smoke. I sat in a chair and Sally folded down on an ottoman. Pancho curled himself in the basket with an ear up for listening.

Sally said, "Did you ever hate any one violently?"

"Of course, Sally."

"A female?"

"Often with women, it's another female, I think."

"She's stinking. I tell myself every day, every hour, that it's not worth it. I go out, do things, get her off my mind. But she doesn't stay off. She comes back, with her little sickly smile. Always, there she is, smiling."

So it was Rosemary, not Amanda, that she hated.

"Is she after Kim, Sally?"

"She's after everybody. She even goes after Iles when Amanda has her back turned. Iles is so sweet and honest he doesn't even know what she's up to!"

Sally got up and got me an ashtray and sat down again.

"Funny thing about man-collectors, Sally. They seldom get a good man for their own. For keeps, I mean."

"She doesn't want one. She had a good man. He was old but she did the snaring. She got the marriage annulled. He let her nick him for three million dollars, if you please."

"Gosh."

"Ever since she's been what she calls independent. But she won't live alone. Not she. And Amanda and Juliana think her pink perfection."

All at once Sally laughed her clear, girlish laugh.

"If I'm not more careful you'll know who I mean, Jean."

"You needn't be careful. She's already trying to latch onto my Pat. Fortunately, she's not his type."

"She's not Kim's either. But she latched. The trouble she's made!"

"How come?"

"She handed him a doughnut." Sally laughed again. "While the rest of us were buckling down to winning the war, Rosemary did her bit in a made-to-order Red Cross uniform." Sally's attractive face grew sober. "I'm talking like a cat. I don't feel nice doing it, either."

"Don't worry about Kim, Sally. She'd much rather hook Lucius Brady."

"Brady?" Sally laughed again. "Two of a kind. He's just as slithery as she is. Oh, what good is money, Jean? For us it has ruined everything. We used to be so happy. We had a wonderful life. And now here we are, parked in this stupid, dull house. Why? Because Iles struck it rich."

"He is proud of Amanda and the house, Sally."

Sally's mouth quivered.

"How mean I am!" she said. "Yes, you are right, and I am ashamed of myself for being so selfish. Iles loves Amanda. And he thinks he loves the house, for her sake. The answer is that I've got to get out of here. Pronto."

Struck by the change in her voice, Pancho left the basket and came and sat beside her. She stroked his smooth coat. The position of his ears changed with every change in her tone.

"He's exactly like Sam," Sally said, giving him a fond smile. "I'll tell you about Sam, Jean. I found him in the creek. I couldn't understand it. Sam was too smart to drown. So I took him to a vet for a post-mortem. He had been poisoned with cyanide."

"Poisoned?"

"Amanda said at first it must have been some neighbor who was annoyed with Sam. That was nonsense. Dachshunds don't annoy anybody. They don't bark unless it's necessary. They patrol the grounds but they don't go bothering the neighbors. Iles said maybe it was a prowler. But Amanda decided then that he was struck by a car, and then drowned. She's stuck to that story. And both Rosemary and Amanda said that, after all, why the fuss, since Sam was only a dog. I said that was exactly why there was a fuss, that there was no real protection for dogs except the kindness of human beings. There are no police to protect dogs. If people love them they are fairly safe. Otherwise not. It's a terrible crime to poison a helpless creature. You could shoot a person for that and it would stand up in court in Texas. "Sally modified that." At least in West Texas," she said.

"Sally, why don't you get a job somewhere?"

"That's my idea. I'm going to West Texas and get a job. We had a wonderful life out there. My mother died when I was tiny and Iles's sister Ann lived with us. She was a lot like Iles. We went wherever he was and lived in whatever we could find to live in. If there was any decent furniture we thought we were lucky. We always made our own curtains, out of muslin or denim, and we had some real silver and nice dishes and our own cooking utensils and linens, and in no time at all Ann and I would make a place home, even though it was just a shack." The bitterness came back. "Now we live like this, have four cars, a private plane, and worry all the time about going broke. It didn't used to make any difference. When we had money we used it. When we didn't, we pulled in our belts. But I liked the life we led then and I'm going back to it."

"With Kim, maybe?"

Sally's voice saddened, and up went Pancho's ears.

"I'm afraid not. Some things you just can't take. Look, I'm talking too much. I don't really blame Amanda for wanting this place. It's her idea of living. She's a town woman. She grew up in Dallas. She thinks life out in the oil fields too uncomfortable and silly for words. But it's Rosemary I'm laying for, and I mean it."

"You don't mean that, Sally."

"No, I guess not. Juliana is alone and she wants Rosemary with her. But Juliana bores Rosemary. Also, there's a man in this house. Gosh, I'm awful."

"No, you aren't, Sally. And you're also a hundred times more attractive than she is."

"No. I'm too long-stemmed."

"Oh, no. You tall gals are the nuts these days. Kim is afraid of Rosemary. Why?"

Sally did not answer.

"How long have you known Kim?"

"Since college. We were together a lot. And then he joined up. And then so did I. They sent me East and Kim stayed ages in Texas before he was shipped out to Japan. We didn't see each other for three years."

"And meanwhile Rosemary handed him a doughnut."

Sally laughed again.

I stood up. "I'll see you tomorrow, Sally. What about Pancho?"

"Oh, Jean, you won't take him away?"

I laughed. "Not if you really want to keep him. He's in luck. Very elegant quarters for a mere visiting dog."

She tucked Pancho under one arm and saw me to the hall door. Suddenly she kissed me on the cheek, and simultaneously Pancho licked my chin. I stepped out into the hall.

As I did, I saw Rosemary, in what looked like a black lacy ensemble, float across the back end of the hall. A door closed.

She had not seen me, I thought. I walked into the main upstairs hall and along the railing which guarded the stairwell and started down the stairs.

I heard an angry voice. I slowed down and kept near the wall.

Amanda said, "You're such a fool!"

"Oh, Sister," Juliana said, in her metallic and now supplicating voice. "Please. I want you to approve, dear."

"Well, I don't. And I never will."

"But it's all right. And it makes me so happy."

"Happy!" Amanda snorted.

"Oh, dear," said Juliana. There were tears in her voice now. "I thought you would be pleased."

"Well, I'm not. You are *not* going to do it, hear?"

There was the sound of a stinging slap. A woman gasped.

I hurried around the newel post and into the living room. Whatever Juliana was not to do, I did not hear.

There was no one in the living room. Above the mantel a portrait of Amanda looked rich and correct. The artist had imitated Gainsborough. A painter in modern style might have caught the chic witchery of Amanda's interesting face. Or he might have been clever and malicious, and with a few twists of his brush, made her look like Juliana.

A door stood open into a little hall which separated the living room and the bar.

The bar was Iles's own spot. On the wood-paneled walls were framed photographs picturing life in the oil fields, gushers and derricks, and groups of working men clustered around pipelines and oil pumps. A collection of guns rested on racks along one wall.

On the high rattan stools, Iles, Patrick and Lucius Brady sat with their highballs. As I entered they stood up. I declined a drink and took a stool and they sat down and resumed their talk. Iles was telling about a new well in Upton County, Texas. It tapped heretofore unimaginable reserves, he said, but the cost of such drilling was not at present practicable.

He seemed relaxed and happy.

A door stood open on the lawn. The moon was shining and I could see a white path winding away into darkness.

4

FIVE MINUTES or so later, Amanda Dollahan came in and told Lucius Brady that Juliana wished to go home. Her face looked pink but otherwise she was perfectly composed.

"Why don't you drive back here after you drop Julie. Lucius?"

Lucius pled a need for sleep, and told us each and all with a gracious formality, goodnight. Iles did not press him to stay.

After Amanda and Brady had gone out his mood changed. He seemed preoccupied and gloomy.

"We must be going, too, Pat."

"Oh, don't go yet," Iles said, quickly. "I've got things to talk over, Pat. You can think about them and we'll continue our talk at breakfast. Is seven too early for you? I want to have plenty of time with you, see, but also I've got to be in Odessa before noon."

Amanda returned, mentioned a headache, and asked if we would excuse her. I said we'd be going as soon as I could break up Pat's and Iles's huddle. She told us goodnight, kissed Iles's cheek, and again left us.

Iles poured himself and Patrick more whisky. I again refused a drink, being anxious to end the party. I longed for a cup of coffee. There was an electric coffee machine behind the bar, but its operation would take time.

I felt oppressed. There was a lot of hate under this roof.

Iles took a fine old cognac from a compartment behind the bar.

"Can't I tempt you with this, Jean?"

I gave in, and had a small jigger in a big crystal glass.

"Not even our friend Brady gets that, Jean. I reckon he thinks maybe I don't know there is such fine liquor. He's got me down as a roughneck that can't do better than tell rye whisky from corn." His deep laugh boomed. "Funny what your women folks fall for, sometimes. That fellow sure takes a mint of money out of Texas."

"Oil money comes easy, Iles," I said.

He gave me a level glance under his thick graying eyebrows. "When it finally comes."

"It must be fun to have it."

"The fun is getting it, honey. It's thinking ahead about what it's going to be like. It's spending it in your mind ahead of time. It's the big money I'm talking about, not just an ordinary strike."

"You sound like your daughter Sally."

"She's a great kid. But it was a tough life for a little girl. She don't remember all the hard knocks. The heat and the dust storms and the scorpions and rattlesnakes. She used to ride her pony across that country and pop the heads off the snakes with a little pistol. Luckily Sally was always quicker than any snake."

At ten minutes past one I said we had to go. Iles had not yet mentioned what he wanted to talk to Patrick · about at breakfast.

He saw us to the car. We left him standing at the end of the flagged walk, a tall and suddenly lonely-looking man, with the moonlight gleaming on his white hair.

"It's going to rain," he called, as we started away.

We moved on in the dappled moonlight.

"He didn't want us to leave, Pat. For some reason or other he didn't want us to go."

"He's got something on his mind."

"Business?"

"I don't know."

"I'll bet it's Lucius Brady. Amanda and Juliana were quarreling tonight. In the dining room. Juliana was standing up to her, too. Until she got slapped."

"Wow!"

"You said Juliana told you why she was so happy tonight?"

"Right."

"Is she going to marry Brady?"

"I told you it was a secret."

"Nothing else could have made their quarrel so fierce."

"Then Amanda's a fool. Iles is a good man. They're scarce."

The winding street ended at a thoroughfare banked with honeysuckle and dense shrubbery. Patrick turned right towards Turtle Creek Boulevard. He stopped on a bridge over the creek. He unlatched the catches which fasten the top to the frame of the windshield.

"It's going to rain, Pat."

"Then we'll put the top up again."

When he pressed the button which lowers the top the extra strain killed the motor. In the sudden quiet the air hummed with the sound of the creek. There seemed to be a sort of dam or waterfall over which the water fell heavily.

Patrick peered out his side of the car.

"There's a big black cloud. We'll leave it up." He fastened the catches and put his arm around me. "Gee, you're nice."

"I am not. I am a very catty woman and an ungrateful guest. I hated this party, Pat."

"Remember the first time I kissed you?"

"Um-m."

"Glad I did?"

"I'll say."

"Me, too."

"You're awfully amorous for some reason."

"Texas, honey. There's a lot of loving in Texas."

"Well, so long as the loved one is me. Did Rosemary make a pass at you when you drove her downtown?"

"Now, sugar. Down here in Texas us men don't talk bad talk about nice little gals."

"Stop kidding, Pat. She's not nice. She's making trouble for Sally. A straight-thinking girl like Sally is no match for one like Rosemary, either."

"Rosemary looks mighty purty and sweet."

"Stop it!"

Patrick laughed and lit a cigarette. "Okay. Spill it!"

"Well, Sally wanted to talk to me. She didn't stay home tonight because of Pancho, but because of some trouble from Rosemary. She wasn't explicit but Rosemary has made trouble between Sally and Kim Forsythe. It happened while he was in the service. Sally knew him first, at the university, but Rosemary latched onto him during the war. Sally said she handed him a doughnut. I guess it was the usual stuff. Glamorous home-girl making hay while the sun shone. Rosemary has money of her own, but she lives by her own choice with the Dollahans. Amanda is for her, of course. Iles is away a lot, I expect, and he just lets the thing slide. Getting around to Sally's dog Sam, he was poisoned. Sally had an autopsy done."

"Who poisoned the dog?"

"She doesn't know. Amanda said at first it might have been a neighbor. But she told us, remember, that he got hit by a car and drowned trying to get home across the creek."

"Anything else?"

"Not specially. Sally was just blowing off steam. And then sorry right away, as nice people are, because she'd done it. She's going to get a job and get out of that house. She was quite nice about Amanda."

"What does *quite* mean?"

"Well, she said she'd hate to be so selfish as not to want her father to be happy. And things like that."

"Do you think he's happy, Jean?"

"On the whole, I would say yes. He seems so proud of everything, including his wife."

Patrick said, "I surmise Iles has been used to honest womenfolk. He probably had a good mother and his sister was on the square. His daughter, also. It would take him a while to get wise to any double-dealing on the part of a wife. A woman gets all the breaks to start with when a man is like Iles. But heaven help her if she does do him dirty, and he finally finds it out."

"Well, it isn't as bad as all that, is it?"

"Iles wouldn't exactly like it if Amanda had poisoned Sally's dog."

"Sally doesn't think it was Amanda. She thinks it was Rosemary."

"Why?"

"I don't know. There's trouble there all around. Look at the way both Rosemary and Amanda walked out on the party. I saw Rosemary just as I left Sally's room. She had changed to a dark outfit. She was crossing the back end of the hall in that wing of the house. I got the feeling that she had started somewhere and had turned back for some reason."

Suddenly above the hum of the waterfall we heard a dog barking hysterically.

I sat up straight.

"That's Pancho!"

"Sounds like him."

"Positive. I wonder what's up?"

"Probably chasing a cat."

The barking stopped abruptly. It had been so frantic the sound had reached us above the noise of the water. It had me worried. I thought about Sam.

"Let's go back for Pancho."

"Look, to find a kennel, at this hour. . . ."

"Pat, we're going back!"

Patrick started the car. We turned right on the boulevard, right again at the next turning, then right again and back along the narrow one-way street.

The house looked just as it had ten or twelve minutes before. The moon shone. Light was showing downstairs in the right wing, through a window which was probably in Iles's bar.

Suddenly a figure came running around the house from the right. It crossed the lighted window. I recognized Sally Dollahan.

She clutched something in her arms.

Patrick was after her instantly. He caught up as Sally reached the service entrance.

"Sally?" he said quietly.

"Oh!" she cried, "Take him, Pat. I shouldn't've kept him in this house. But I was so careful. I waited to take him out until I thought they were in bed. But he yanked himself free. Somebody was there."

The leash dangled from his collar. Patrick was running expert fingers over the dog.

"Where did you find him, Sally?"

"At the foot of the terrace steps. Almost in the creek. His leash had caught on the railing or he would have been washed away. Whoever it was tried to drown him."

"He's all right."

Patrick handed the wet dog to me.

He dashed around the house in the direction from which Sally had come. I moved as fast as I could with ten pounds of wet brown dog. I could feel Pancho's heart beating along in its usual healthy dog fashion.

Sally stayed with me. She was crying now, not making much noise but crying as hysterically as the dog had been barking a few minutes ago.

We passed the outside door of Iles's bar. It was closed. On around the house we came to the short wide flight of stone steps which led from the lawn to the terrace parallel with the creek. The moon was under the black cloud. It was hard to see and, carrying the dog, I walked slowly. Sally went ahead. Patrick had disappeared in darkness. Something glinted on one of the terrace steps. Shifting the dog to one arm, I stooped and picked up a piece of jewelry. I dropped it in my bag, a complex operation, because Pancho was reviving and ready to continue the chase.

Suddenly lights came on. Patrick blinked as he came up the steps at the other end of the terrace.

The door opened. Iles Dollahan stepped out.

"Thought you folks had left?"

"We heard the dog, and came back."

"Oh, Iles!" Sally cried. "Somebody tried to kill Pancho."

"I reckon it wasn't that bad, honey," Iles said.

I handed the squirming dog to Patrick. Iles was damned complacent. I was angry for another reason too. My beautiful best outfit was generously spotted now with water Pancho had acquired in Turtle Creek.

"Where's Rosemary?" Sally demanded.

Iles said, "She's upstairs. I saw her just now as I was going up to bed. Then I heard you all walking around so I came down to see what was up. Is the dog all right, Pat?"

"Yes," Patrick said. "Just a conk on the noggin. Just missed an eye, though."

Sally faced Iles. She was shaking with hysterical anger.

"This time, if you don't do something, I will. Sam was murdered. I told you so. You didn't believe me. This time . . ."

"Now, listen, Sally, maybe somebody was prowling . . ."

"That's what you said before. But this time it's Jean's dog. We're responsible. We have to do something."

"It's all right, Sally," I said.

Patrick set the dog down. Pancho whimpered and strained at the leash. Patrick let the dog draw him down the steps along a flagstone walk which followed the creek.

"Hey?" Iles called. "I wouldn't go on there if I was you, Pat."

Patrick went on, guided by the dog. They disappeared around a great forsythia bush.

Iles turned suddenly, and without another word stepped inside, fastened the door, and snapped off the terrace lights.

"I'm following Pat, Sally," I said.

"I'll come too."

We found our way in thick darkness. We rounded the big clump of forsythia. Patrick was on ahead. In the darkness I let Sally go first. We were near the edge of the grounds when not six steps away Patrick turned his pocket flashlight on a dark thing on the bank. It looked like a sprawl of dark clothing.

"It's Rosemary!" Sally cried out.

Patrick handed me the dog's leash and stooped to pull the woman's head out of the creek. He turned her over.

The moon came out. I could see Sally Dollahan's face as she stared at the woman on the grassy bank. It was stiff and incredulous.

"There has been some mistake," she said.

5

A BLACK cloud again crossed the moon. We stood in shadow. The moving water glistened, and the butterfly blossoms of the forsythia seemed to float further away. The dark thing on the creek's bank merged with the darkness of grass and shrub.

Sally said, "It must be Rosemary. She came upstairs and changed to a dark outfit. The water may have made her hair dark."

"Not water entirely. There's blood." Patrick's voice was angry. I could see his face, cold and angry and puzzled. I knew the woman must be dead.

"Blood?" I said.

Patrick said, "What makes you think it is Rosemary, Sally?"

Sally's behavior, for a girl who was crying like a child a few minutes before, was remarkably calm.

"Wishful thinking, I suppose."

"Be careful, Sally. This could be murder."

Patrick sounded clinical, but still angry, as he stood up and said, "It's Juliana Willoz. She's been shot. Jean, go and find a phone and notify the police." Then he said, "No, I'll go. You stay here with Sally."

Sally got upset again.

"I won't stay here," she declared.

"Why not?"

"I'm sorry," Sally said. "I know I sounded odd when I spoke as I did, and for insisting it was Rosemary. But I won't stay here. I must see my father, at once."

"Why?"

"Because he saw Rosemary upstairs a few minutes ago. There must have been some mistake."

"Apparently," Patrick said drily. "Okay. Give me the dog, Jean, and go with Sally. Call the police. You know what to say."

The black clouds overhead had thickened. We had to walk slowly again because of the darkness. The door leading from the bar was locked, so we walked around to the service entrance, talking in whispers as we moved.

"What made you think it was Rosemary, Sally?"

"Because she's always asking for trouble, I guess." Her tone was bitter.

"You mustn't say such things. This may be murder."

"Nobody would murder Juliana, poor thing."

"Apparently somebody did."

"Then it was an accident. Anyway, it wasn't me did it, Jean."

"Nobody said it was, Sally. But you were outside when it happened."

"I don't think I was."

"Didn't you hear a shot?"

"No, I did not. But I should have heard a shot if I had been outside at the time. The creek is making a lot of noise and so are the frogs, but you would have heard the shot above that sort of racket. If the gun was fired near our house."

The frogs had begun to warble again. Those nearby had kept quiet while we had the lights on, when we were on the terrace, and while Patrick was using the flashlight along the creek. Once more they were filling the night with their foolish trills and bellows.

From a short hall inside the service entrance the service stairs led up to the wing which included Sally's bedroom. Rosemary's too, as we were to learn. On the ground floor a door opened from the hall into the kitchen. There was a telephone on a small desk near a door from the kitchen into the pantry.

"This phone is out of order," Sally said. "We'll use the one in the bar."

A voice stopped us as we were entering the bar. The room itself was dark.

"Who is it?"

It was Iles Dollahan speaking. His voice was thick and confused.

"It's me, dear." Sally spoke gently. "We've got to use the phone, Iles. Something awful has happened. Juliana has been—hurt."

"She's dead," I said.

"What do you mean, dead?" Iles growled.

"Well, she is," Sally said. "She's up by the creek. Dead. Pat thinks she's been shot."

Sally touched a switch that turned on the concealed lighting of the attractive room. Iles was leaning against the bar. Near his right hand was what looked like a half-tumbler of straight whisky. The guns I had noted previously all rested on their racks on the wood-paneled walls.

I said, "We've got to call the police."

"Oh, no." Dollahan's eyes under their straight thick brows were gray and cruel. "No, you don't call no police. I ain't going to have the law bothering around here."

"But you'll have to," I said. "This is murder, Iles."

"Oh, no, I don't have to. No police, see? Just you wait till I finish the drink and I'll go and talk to Pat about the way to handle this. I'm not going to have the police nosing around here."

He was drunk. There was no use arguing. Sally said nothing, and I waited.

Iles took a long drink. "There's some mistake. Juliana went home a good while ago." He finished the drink and got a glass of water. "I'll go and talk to Pat. We'll fix things up among ourselves, see. Just take it easy for a minute and then I'll see Pat."

I had a brain wave.

"Sally, I'll run back and tell Pat not to do anything till they have talked it over."

Sally made a move towards the outside door.

"You can go out this way, Jean."

"I'll go the way we came in." I walked back through the living room, across the hall, into the dining room, and through the butler's pantry to the kitchen. There I grabbed the phone.

The operator answered at once.

"The police," I said. "Homicide."

Immediately the connection was made, I gave my message and cradled the phone. Sally spoke behind me.

"That was a dirty trick!"

"I was obeying Pat's orders."

"You tricked my father. It was a low-down thing to do."

Without another word she turned her back and left me.

I left the house feeling miserable and angry.

"I thought you were never coming!" Patrick said.

"Iles tried to interfere."

"He did, huh? Here, take Pancho. Keep him quiet, mind. Here are the car keys. Take the dog in the car and wait for me on the bridge by the waterfall."

"But the police. . . ."

"Do as I say! Hurry!"

Waiting on the bridge by the waterfall . . . or the dam if you prefer . . . had been romantic a few minutes ago. Now I sat numbly, but not for long, for in two minutes I heard a siren and the first police car appeared and ran through the red blinker at the intersection of this street with the boulevard. It went straight on, slowing for the turning which would lead into the one-way street which passed the Dollahan house.

A second car followed. As its taillights vanished rain began to fall suddenly and heavily. I turned on the windshield wipers. The motor was idling. The wipers swung back and forth with a mechanical flip-flop.

The dog pressed against me for comfort. He had a blanket in the back seat. I twisted to get it and whirled back into my seat as the car door opened. My heart was beating like mad.

Pancho's tail was wagging. It was Patrick.

"You scared me to death!" I said.

"Whew!" he said. "Get going. Turn left at the blinker and I'll direct you as we go."

We were already moving. I made the stop at the blinker, turned left and followed Turtle Creek Boulevard.

"Where are we going, Pat?"

"To the Adolphus."

"Why?"

"I want to get hold of Kim Forsythe."

"Oh?" Patrick didn't crash through with any information so I said, "Did you get very wet?"

"No. I was waiting under a tree till the patrol cars passed. I left Dollahan's almost as soon as you did. I didn't want to be seen leaving. Also I wanted to get the lay of the land on this side of the house. They'll spend time looking for me, too, which I can use looking for Kim."

"You don't think Kim . . ."

Patrick said, "Angle off here under the viaduct. Isn't it marvelous how a dog gets over things? Operate on one and he's up and about in an hour. Knock him out, and . . ."

"Pat, stop it! Why do you want to see Kim? Either Iles did it, or Sally."

"Why?"

"From the way Sally behaved. And Iles, too. Iles was busy getting drunk. Sally tried to keep me from phoning the police. There's an extension in the kitchen. She said it was out of order and took me to the bar. Iles was there, drinking straight whisky."

"You're sure it was straight whisky?"

"Oh, Pat. I'm not, of course. But it looked it. Anyway, there was Iles, in the dark, having a solitary drink. He said straight off he didn't want the police called. He said he'd talk to you first. He stalled and got a glass of water. So I pretended to be coming back to tell you what he'd said and stopped and called the police from the kitchen phone. It wasn't out of order. Sally lied. And she followed me and when I hung up she said I'd played her father a dirty trick. I feel awful."

"Iles is used to running his own shows, Jeanie."

"What makes you say that?"

"Turn left at the second red blinker."

"Okay. What made you say . . ."

"Well, under his gentle exterior Iles Dollahan is a very tough hombre. He's lived in a tough world. He has, incidentally, killed people before."

"Before? Then you think . . ."

"Two men. In self-defense, I believe."

I shuddered.

Patrick said, "Out on a lease. But this is Dallas, not a lonely oil lease in West Texas, and it was your duty to call the police."

"I'm afraid Sally will never like me again, Pat."

"Hey! Red blinker!"

I slammed on the brakes, signaled, and made the turning.

"You said Juliana had been shot. I took a look at those guns on the walls in the bar. They were all there."

Patrick chuckled.

"If the Dollahans wanted to go gunning they wouldn't have to resort to their souvenirs, Jean. No rain fell here. None fell apparently from about three blocks this side of the viaduct."

The clouds had passed over and the moon was shining again when we stepped out of the car in front of the hotel. The pavement was dry. Patrick tucked Pancho under one arm. We stopped at the desk for the key. Nobody made any objection to the dog. The clerk handed out the key, and said nothing. In the big leather chairs beside the baskets of spiky greenery opposite the desk, three men with bronzed skins and small Stetsons talked together, giving the otherwise unpeopled lobby a feeling of life. We took the elevator up to our floor. The operator said what a cute dog, and we agreed.

"Well, I guess they don't mind," I said, as we walked along the hall towards our rooms. "There may be a ruling in this hotel against dogs, but in Texas they hate to remind you of a ruling."

Patrick snapped off Pancho's leash and set him free. Straight away he started investigating everything, sniffing at each object as if he meant to know all that had happened to it.

The telephone sounded brusquely.

"Oh, dear! The police already," I said.

Patrick said, "Hello? . . . Oh, yes, but we're going right out again. yes, we do know. . . . Good night."

He cradled the receiver. He was smiling.

"House detective," he said. "Dogs are not allowed."

He took up the phone and asked for Kim Forsythe's room. Kim answered at once. Patrick asked if he would mind coming to our rooms. Kim asked why, and Patrick said please to come at once, that it was a matter of urgent importance.

Kim was on our floor, further along the hall. He knocked on our door within half a minute. He was dressed as we had last seen him. His hair and the shoulders of his jacket were wet.

We had not yet sat down. Kim stood, his eyes puzzled.

Patrick said, "You got rained on?"

Kim smiled his shy, winning smile.

"I say. But I was lucky and picked up a cab before I was soaked through."

"Where were you at the time?"

"Don't ask me. Somewhere between here and the Dollahans."

"Did you come directly here?"

"What do you mean?"

"Follow the way we took when we drove back there tonight?"

"No. I had never walked it before and I got off the course. Not that it made any difference."

"It might," Patrick said. "Remember the number of your cab? Or the driver?"

Kim stiffened. "Hey, what is this?"

"One of the Willoz sisters has been murdered." Kim turned livid under his tan. He could hardly speak. He left the door and came close to where we stood near the middle of the room. Then he said, "Not . . . Rosemary?"

"That's funny," Patrick said. "Sally said the same thing."

"Who was it?" Kim demanded harshly.

"Juliana," Patrick said. "Sit down, Kim. The police will be after us all, *muy pronto*, and we might as well sit it out together. Why did you think it might be Rosemary?"

Kim took out his cigarettes. His hand trembled.

"Wishful thinking, I guess."

"Just what Sally said," I said.

Kim gave me a vague glance and then said, "I hate to talk against a woman, but when they do the things Rosemary does, you can't always stick to the rules, can you? She's a devil and it's no wonder if she gets herself murdered."

"You had trouble with Rosemary?"

"Plenty."

"Care to tell me about it?"

"Why should I?" Kim gave Patrick a hard, straight, gray glance. "Did you say Juliana? Must have been an accident or something."

Patrick said. "She was shot through the head. On the bank of the creek. She was still dressed in the clothes she wore last evening. But her slippers looked scuffed, as if she had been walking where it was rough. The police are there now. We came back here to see you. To warn you, I should say."

Kim moved to his right, and sat down. Pancho had been sniffing around his feet. He left him to explore behind a sofa.

"It must have been an accident," Kim said again, wearily.

"Why?"

"Well, Juliana was so nice. Not very interesting, but nice. I know her ex-husband. He's out in Odessa. He's always been sorry about the divorce and he wanted her back. He made a pile of money in a big strike around six months ago and I happen to know he's been after Juliana to marry him again."

"Did she tell you?"

"He told me. He told me other things, too."

"Care to pass them along?"

"Certainly not," Kim said. "What's it got to do with you?"

"Nothing," Patrick said. "But if you happen to need any help, Kim, and I can give it, let me know. You don't like Rosemary Willoz. At least you're definite about that."

"I certainly don't."

"What's the name of Juliana's ex-husband?"

"Green. Ulysses B. What has that got to do with this?"

"Nothing, maybe. Did you have a date to meet Rosemary tonight after you left the Dollahans?"

Kim's gray eyes widened. Then they went blank.

"Look here, Pat. When I need what you call help I'll let you know. Meanwhile mind your own business."

"All right," Patrick said. "But one more thing, if you don't mind. How did you leave the house?"

"By the door on the terrace."

"Where's your topcoat?"

"I forgot it there. I've got to phone Iles to fetch it in the morning."

"Did you walk around the house and use the street?"

"Why, of course. What other way is there?"

"Then which way did you walk?"

Kim frowned, but replied. "I walked along that narrow street in front of the house till I came to a wider cross street, turned right, crossed the creek by a bridge near a dam, and turned left at the traffic light on Turtle Creek Boulevard. I walked on and came to a sort of park. I don't remember going through this part when we drove to the house. I'm not well acquainted with Dallas. It began to rain about the time I got to another boulevard. I caught a cab there."

"See anybody who would remember seeing you?" Kim looked puzzled. He asked again, "Remember your cab? Or the driver?"

"What is all this, anyhow?"

A light knock sounded on the hall door.

"That house detective," I said.

Pancho's long face appeared between the sofa and the wall. His ears were up for listening.

"Come in," Patrick called.

The door opened and in stepped Iles Dollahan. He closed the door quietly. From his right hand pocket he took out and leveled on Patrick a big black automatic.

"I'll thank you for that red horse," he said.

6

IN THE strange cold clarity fear sometimes brings I stood watching the little black hole in the big black automatic pistol.

He, Iles Dollahan, has killed two men, I was thinking. They called it self-defense.

Beneath that big white-haired gently-spoken exterior he is ruthless.

His daughter, Sally, with her little face and clear green eyes, is like him.

So— but in a different fashion—is Amanda. So is Rosemary. So is Lucius Brady. They're a bunch of tough guys, all right. *Muy* tough. All but Juliana. And Juliana is dead.

"You heard me," Iles Dollahan said.

His voice had a poisonous softness.

"Sure," Patrick said. He was standing relaxed, with his hands sticking up idly, in a silly sort of way. Between his lips a cigarette smoked languorously. "But I really don't know what you're talking about, Iles."

"My wife dropped a red horse. On the terrace. I came after it and I don't aim to leave till I get it."

Oh, I thought. I felt faint. It was in my bag. It was the thing that glinted, in the moonlight, and which I picked up and slid into my bag.

I reached for my bag, which was on a chair behind me.

"Don't move, ma'am," Iles said. That ma'am was as curt as a bullet.

"For God's sake, Iles!" Kim Forsythe said.

"Shut up! "Iles said. He kept watching Patrick but he took a short step backwards, so that the automatic covered us all with hair-raising efficiency. "Okay, Pat. Hand it over!"

Patrick said, with revolting composure, "What makes you think I've got the red horse?"

My palms felt wet. My throat was tight. I couldn't've uttered better than a croak.

"You've got it."

"I'm afraid not."

"You know what I mean, all right. That horse."

Patrick said, "My kingdom for a flying red horse."

My blood ran slow and cold. What a time to joke!

"Cut the smart stuff, Pat. You've got one of those red horses that belong to my wife. You were the first to come up those side steps to the terrace and that is where she says she dropped it."

"Then your wife was on the terrace about the time of the murder?"

Iles looked so murderous at that word murder that I managed to find my voice.

"Iles, I've got it. It's in my bag."

"Why didn't you say so?"

"I was too scared. Put that gun away. I'm too scared to move, with a gun pointing at me."

"It won't go off, ma'am," Iles said softly. "Get me the horse."

I kept watching the little black hole in the gun.

"Shall I, Pat?"

"Certainly," Patrick said. "After all, it isn't our horse. But remind me after this to be careful about where we accept invitations to dinner, dear."

Iles winced. But without taking his eyes off Patrick and keeping us all under cover of that gun, he said, "Give it here, ma'am. Quick."

I managed to reach for my bag, and I began poking feverishly around among its contents for the flying red ruby horse. After what seemed forever my fingers touched it and drew it into my palm. I took my hand out of the bag and pressed the catch which closed it. I set the bag down on the chair. I turned to give the horse to Dollahan.

At that moment a slight movement distracted me.

Close to the floor and to the right of the hall door, dark and sleek and silent as a shadow, our low-slung long-drawn-out Pancho was inching forward. He crouched to attack.

I said, to give the dog time, "I would have given this to you at the house, but I forgot it, Iles. You're lucky these rubies aren't emeralds or I'd probably have kept it always."

Pancho shot through the air and fastened his teeth in Iles Dollahan's left calf.

It was a lovely sight.

"Good dog, Pancho!" I cried.

Iles yelped and looked down. Patrick leaped forward and Kim Forsythe moved in from Iles's right and the two of them took over. Kim took the gun. He put on the safety catch and dropped the big automatic into his pocket. Meanwhile I slipped the ruby horse down into the chair where I'd left my bag, thrusting the clip between the cushion and the side upholstery. Taking my time, I then detached Pancho from Iles Dollahan.

Iles was as good as manacled in the hands of two husky young men. He cussed soundly, and then calmed down.

"Sorry, ma'am," he said, remembering me. "Let me go, boys. You've got me now you've got the gun. But I've got to have that horse. Amanda had nothing to do with her sister's death, Pat. She just happened to step out on the terrace, and she dropped the horse. She discovered it was gone about the time you and Jean left the first time, and then I couldn't find it."

Iles gave me a reproachful look. "You ought to have left it at the house, ma'am."

I said, "How could anybody remember that silly clip? After what I'd seen on the bank of the creek. And after the way you and Sally acted when I tried to phone the police. The horse was nothing, compared to all that awfulness. You ought to be ashamed, bothering about a foolish piece of jewelry at a time like this."

Iles said stubbornly, "The police are going to make us a lot of trouble. You oughtn't've called the police, ma'am." He started rubbing his leg. "Sharp teeth that dog's got!"

Patrick said, "See if you haven't got some iodine or something, Jean. Roll up your pants leg, Iles."

I fetched iodine from my cosmetic case and arrived as Iles finished rolling up one trousers leg, revealing startlingly white flesh for a man with such a deeply tanned face and hands.

On the leg were two sets of identical tooth marks. One, lower down, had not broken the skin. The second, and newest, was slightly bleeding.

I said, "It was you. It was you who kicked Pancho and tried to drown him in the creek!"

Kim took the iodine. Iles made me no answer.

"I'll say, sharp teeth," Kim said.

"You can be glad he's had his rabies shot," Patrick said. "But you'd better see a doctor anyway, Iles."

"Why did you do it?" I insisted. "Why did you kick him down the steps like that? He might have drowned."

"Now, ma'am," Iles said, with humility. "Now, listen, ma'am, I never meant to hurt your dog. He came on me like lightning. In the dark. He grabbed me and I kicked him off. He came at me again and I kicked harder than I meant to. He was only on the steps for a minute, before Sally came around and got him. I would have picked him up if she hadn't."

"And what were you doing there?" I asked.

"I was looking for Amanda's horse."

"There seems to have been a great burst of activity around your house immediately after we left," Patrick said. "Sally said she saw no one on the terrace when she went around there to collect the dog."

Iles continued to be humble.

"I'd stepped back inside. I didn't want her to know I'd hurt the little fellow. She still feels so bad about her own dog. I reckon I was a little drunk, too. I'd had too much whisky for my own good, I reckon. I stepped back in the house and then I heard you all talking so I turned on the lights because I wanted to get the red horse. It cost a pile of money. My wife is crazy about those horses, Pat."

"Why didn't you say you were looking for the horse?"

"Well, you were upset about the dog. So was I. I hated to have hurt the little fellow. I ought to have said so."

He paused. After a moment Patrick said. "Is that all?"

"I reckon so. I know it looks kind of peculiar, but that is the God's truth. I'm sorry about the little dog."

"I guess Pancho's even," I said. "I hope your leg hurts you a lot, Mr. Dollahan, but I don't want you to get hydrophobia, because you would blame that on Pancho. But I'm glad he bit you. Pancho's no joke when he means business. He'll take on a porcupine or a rattlesnake or—"

"If you're calling me a rattlesnake, ma'am . . ."

"She's only saying that Pancho's ambition exceeds his size," Patrick said. "The truth is, he overdoes things. He weighs less than ten pounds but he wouldn't hesitate to take on a flock of lions and as Jean said, with a dozen or so rattlesnakes thrown in. But I wish he could talk. Pancho knows who killed Juliana Willoz."

"How so?"

"Because he hears and smells far more accurately than human beings. I suspect he got excited and jerked his leash away from Sally because he smelled blood. He dashed around the house to attack the murderer and . . . tangled with you."

"Now, you listen here!" Iles said. "Give me that horse. And stop talking double talk. I've got to get back to the house."

"How did you get away?"

"Walked. Got a cab over on McKinney. I heard those police sirens, and I didn't have time to get out my car, or I'd've been here ahead of you. What about that horse?"

Patrick said, "Give it to him, Jean."

I stepped over and tried to find it where I had put it in beside the cushion of the chair. I was still holding the dog. The clip had gone further down than I expected, and I was a minute or so finding it. Then I handed it to Patrick, who held it up and looked at it under the glowing ceiling light.

"Very pretty, Iles."

Sweat was standing on Iles's forehead.

"It ought to be. Those damn things set me back fifteen thousand bucks. You know anything about jewelry, Pat? Amanda says the things were a bargain, but it's hard to think of anybody getting a bargain out of Lucius Brady."

Patrick stepped back a step, to allow the light to play differently upon the charming treasure. "Iles, after you shut and locked the door on the terrace, why did you go to your bar and take a stiff drink? All by yourself, in the dark?"

"That's none of your business!"

"Of course not. But you'd better be thinking up a nice answer, because the police are going to ask you that, too."

"They won't know about it."

"They'll question Jean. She knows about it."

"If it's money you want, Abbott . . ."

"Money? God forbid. I merely want satisfaction for my client."

"Client?"

Patrick jerked a hand at the dog.

"Pancho. Pancho del Rio. Who narrowly escaped losing his life because you kicked him in the head."

"Now, you see here!" Iles began.

A soft rap sounded on the door. Iles rolled down his pants leg. I said, "Come in."

A moon-faced man opened the door and looked in. He looked apologetic.

"Hate to disturb you folks. I'm the house detective. You won't forget to take your dog away, will you?"

"No," Patrick said. "Thank you."

"Thank *you*, sir. Well, good night, all."

"Good night," we all said, except Iles Dollahan.

The man closed the door. Patrick took out his cigarettes.

"Gave me kind of a scare," he said lightly. He loosened a cigarette from the pack with one hand. In the other he still held the ruby horse. "I thought he was the homicide squad."

Iles stood up, tall, taller than Kim, taller even than Patrick.

"Give me the horse. I've got to get back and try to explain where I've been. Would appreciate it if you say I've been here, Pat. That is, if the police ask you. Say I came on business."

"Sure, and why not?" Patrick said.

There was another light tap, and this time Patrick bade the visitor enter. But even before he had issued the invitation the door opened. In walked a man with a brown complexion, shiny black eyes and shiny white teeth. His hair under the old brown hat on the back of his head was black and shining. He wore a wrinkled brown suit. Behind him came two larger men, in the uniform of the Dallas police force.

The detective said, "Which of you is John McKim Forsythe?" Kim stepped forward. "Okay, boys." The two men in uniform worked Kim over and handed the detective the big automatic. "Didn't even bother to get rid of it, huh?" He checked the safety catch and, wrapping it in his handkerchief, said, "All of you come along with us."

7

PATRICK gave me a glance which I took correctly as a request to stall for time. I asked if I might change my dampish clothes and the police detective, whose name was Raymond Tisbury, a detective lieutenant of the Dallas police department, nodded consent. Kim and Iles went with Tisbury. I picked up Pancho's leash and took him with me into the bedroom, where I got out of my glad rags, hoping they would clean well, and into a gray flannel suit and a black shantung blouse. I was tying a black silk scarf around my hair when I heard Patrick's voice in the sitting room.

I stepped over to the night stand and took up the telephone.

"Odessa operator?" Patrick asked. "I want to talk with a man named Green. Ulysses B. Green. He's in the oil business, I believe."

"Who isn't, out here?" giggled the operator. She took a moment, and then said, in an awed tone, "I'm sorry, sir. He's dead."

"Dead?"

"Yes, sir. He died early yesterday morning."

"What of?"

"Why, I don't know, Personally, I wasn't acquainted."

"Know his doctor?"

"No, sir."

"Well, find him. No, just call the leading doctor in the place and let me talk to him."

"I wouldn't know which . . ."

"Call any doctor who has a good practice."

I listened in, breathless, even after Patrick said, "Getting an earful, Jeanie? Okay, as long as it doesn't weaken the connection. If it does, you hang up."

I said okay just as a sleepy voice growled, "Dr. Hepbourne speaking?"

Patrick said brazenly, "This is the police department in Dallas, Dr. Hepbourne. Did you happen to have a patient named Green? Ulysses B. Green?"

"I guess you'd call him my patient," the doctor growled. "They called me in just when he kicked off. I'd never seen him professionally before then."

"What ailed him?"

"Oh, something he ate. These oil men eat everything from shoe leather to armadillos and think nothing of it. It gets them sooner or later."

"Was there an autopsy?"

"Autopsy?" the doctor said. "What for?"

"He may have been murdered."

"Rats. What for? He didn't leave chick nor child. Nothing but a grass widow who didn't give a hoot for him. I might add he hadn't even an enemy. You might say no friends, either. Solitary guy. They get like that out in the oil fields."

"I understand he was pretty well fixed?"

"So what?" the doctor said.

"You mean he wasn't?"

"I mean I doctored him. Wasn't his banker."

"Well, thanks," Patrick said. "We'll get in touch with your local police, Doctor."

"Wish you'd done it in the first place. Need my sleep."

"I'm sorry."

"Oh, that's all right. So long."

Patrick said good-bye and cradled his receiver and I stepped out into the sitting room.

"What made you do that, Pat?"

"There has to be a motive for murder. I was curious about Ulysses B. Green. And he's dead. Suddenly and recently dead. I wonder if anybody at the Dollahans' knew that? It would be interesting to know who was his heir, in case he died rich. Kim said he wanted to marry Juliana again."

Pancho was listening, intently.

"What do we do with this animal, Pat?"

"Take him with us. No time to find him a kennel now."

As we left the elevator in the lobby the three bronzed men with the small Stetsons were still holding their animated conversation. Standing in an attitude of waiting near the top of the stairs was a stunning woman with red hair and blue-rimmed glasses. She was dressed to the nines in sports clothes, as if she were going to the country.

I glanced at the clock. It was twenty minutes to three A.M.

"How they do it beats me," I said.

"Do what?"

"Look like that, at this hour. Or any hour. Everybody in Dallas looks stylish around the clock, apparently."

"Tut, tut. No time now to discuss the fashions, Jean."

Outside the streets were clean and the wind was blowing and above us the flying red horse was turning slowly around. In the cavernous street between the lofty hotels and office buildings you had the feeling you get in Chicago or New York of being hemmed in by the metropolis. Even when you left this area, which you did by car in a matter of a couple of minutes, the metropolitan feeling went with you.

There were very few pedestrians and fewer automobiles on the streets. The sky had cleared and the moon shone and the air was full of a moist freshness. The smell of spring when we were again along the overflowing creek brought back sharply to mind the tragic corpse of Juliana Willoz.

"I guess I shouldn't have brought this dog, Pat."

"Don't be silly. He's our hero. Except for Pancho the killer of Juliana Willoz would go on record as some prowling homicidal maniac."

"Why so?"

"The body wouldn't've been discovered until daylight. By that time, what with the rain, any chance of picking up the murderer would be pretty much lost."

"May have been any way."

"Yes. But at least an inquiry began almost at once."

"Pat, did Iles Dollahan kill her?"

"If so, why?"

Motives, I thought. Jealousy. Rage. Greed. Revenge. None clicked.

"He admitted kicking our dog. A man who would kick a dog . . ."

"Wait a minute. Who wouldn't kick off a dog whose teeth were buried in his leg? However, Iles undoubtedly was behaving in what Pancho thought was a suspicious manner. Iles was pussyfooting around the terrace looking for the flying red horse in the moonlight. Why didn't he turn on the terrace lights in the first place?"

"Of course. Why didn't he?"

"Maybe because he, or Amanda, or both, didn't want it known that she had been outside and had dropped the red horse. Sally was taking the dog out. They didn't want Sally's attention drawn to Iles's reason for being on the terrace."

"But Pancho again attacked Iles in the hotel."

"That was entirely different. Iles was threatening us and Pancho knew we were frightened. So he attacked. That's simply instinct. He's our dog and he protected us. But I figure he smelled Juliana's blood when he went outside the Dollahans' with Sally. So he yanked the leash from her hand, dashed around the house, saw Iles behaving in what Pancho and even ourselves would think a peculiar way. He grabbed Iles's leg and got kicked down the terrace steps. Too, *too* bad he can't talk."

"You're doing a pretty good job for him, Patrick. Look, if Sally Dollahan shot Rosemary Willoz, or rather shot Juliana thinking her Rosemary, Iles would cover up for her till doomsday."

"Right."

"I admire that, Pat."

"So do I. Only, it isn't exactly right. Well, one thing we know for sure—since he afterwards went to the trouble to come to the hotel to collect it with a gun, Iles was definitely outside to get the red horse. The questions are, was Amanda on the terrace, and if so, why, and why didn't she go after the red horse herself?"

"That gun! It was Kim's!"

"Apparently. He had a gun with him in his topcoat pocket this evening. Remind me, by the way, to give Amanda the red horse. When the police showed up I dropped it in my pocket. Hate to be carrying such an expensive gadget."

We stopped at the red blinker near the waterfall, as Patrick insisted on calling the dam.

"I feel sorry for Iles, Pat. That Amanda, with her ridiculous way of talking and her artificial manners. . . ."

"It's a free country, chum. If Amanda wants to polish herself, why not?"

"You're right. Oh, look across the creek. The Dollahan place looks like Christmas."

There were lights in all the windows and all over the grounds. Those on the terrace were reflected in the creek. Patrick slowed down.

I said, "The reason I'm sorry for Iles, and for Sally, too, is that they are basically honest people. They're no match for slick women like Amanda and Rosemary. And they're fearless. They'll do what they think right regardless, as long as personal loyalties are not involved. I said that Iles would stand by Sally till doomsday. Sally would do the same for Iles. Sally can shoot. If she mistook Juliana for Rosemary. . . ."

"Why not Amanda?" Patrick asked. "Haven't you noticed that Sally doesn't like Amanda?"

He turned off into the one-way street and pulled up short as a flashlight waved in front of us. A uniformed policeman stepped out, asked where we were going, and who we were. He waved us on. The curb was lined with cars, most of them police cars. There was an ambulance from the Parkland Hospital. A Nichols Brothers cab was moving away and Patrick eased into the space it left vacant. Standing on the main walk with Lieutenant Tisbury was Lucius Brady. His greeting for us was without words, but his manner said everything. He displayed his amazement, his horror, and his grief in the way his graceful body drooped and by the movement of his eloquent hands.

8

"BUT Amanda's dress was *white?*" I said, answering with a question Patrick's remark of some minutes before. Maybe she had more than one dress, Patrick said, and then he murmured to shush and I noticed that, without showing the slightest interest, he was eaves-dropping on Lieutenant Tisbury, who was talking to Lucius Brady. Why had Brady taken Mrs. Willoz's car? Because of the lateness of the hour, Brady said. Mrs. Willoz was to have picked it up, he said, tomorrow morning, or he would have fetched it back, either of which arrangement would be made on the telephone. It took a little time, naturally, to get a taxicab at this time of night. Mrs. Willoz and Mrs. Dollahan were old friends. They frequently very kindly accommodated Lucius Brady with an automobile for his use when he was in Dallas. In this, of course, Lieutenant Tisbury—as would anyone else in a country where the automobile is the principal means of transportation,—saw nothing strange.

There were at that time no more questions, Tisbury said, and Brady thanked him and asked him if he might go along and offer his sympathy to Mrs. Dollahan and Miss Willoz. Permission granted, he went ahead, entering and walking through the brightly lighted hall in the direction of the living room.

Tisbury was in fine fettle. His eyes danced like big black-widow spiders. His white teeth gleamed in his brown face.

"Needn't've dragged you folks back here, I reckon."

"You couldn't've kept us away," I said.

Tisbury's glance was genial, but firm. He could have kept us away, and we certainly knew it, his black eyes said. He was the law. Period.

And he was feeling good, so he did not indulge in any verbal contradiction to my announcement.

He thinks the case is sewed up, I thought. He thinks he knows who did the killing. It's Kim! He's going to arrest Kim Forsythe. Maybe he's already arrested him. Poor Sally. My heart hurt for her. I had forgotten already that she had lied and had accused me of tricking Iles. I would have done the same, in her place.

"We've picked up some very conclusive evidence," Tisbury said. "And Miss Rosemary Willoz is making a statement." Patrick looked inquiring and Tisbury said, "She's made one already but this one is for the record."

I said, "Don't believe everything you hear, Lieutenant."

Tisbury grinned exultantly.

"Lady, you're telling me?"

Patrick asked for, and obtained, permission to listen to Rosemary's statement, and, after announcing genially that we sure had a cute dog, Lieutenant Tisbury let us enter the brightly illuminated hall. We walked slowly and, like Brady, towards the door leading to the living room.

Amanda's house obviously absorbed its invaders. In the ice-green perfection of the living room, where the lamps kept the lighting in a subdued yet cool glow, even Lieutenant Tisbury behaved with a slightly refrigerated decorum. Sergeant Isaac Gomez, stenographer and recorder for the detective-lieutenant, had set up a card table and had arranged his notebook and pencils in apple-pie order for taking down evidence in shorthand. He was ready when we entered the room. We sat down near the hall door. Amanda Dollahan and Rosemary Willoz were sitting on one sofa. Lucius Brady sat opposite, smoking one of his Egyptian cigarettes. The condolences had apparently been concluded. Spiritually speaking, Brady already wore a black band on his beautifully tailored sleeve. Amanda looked harried. Rosemary, sobbing effectively, rested her face upon Amanda's shoulder.

Rosemary wore the black ensemble, which was a negligee of black lace over what could be a black sheer nightgown. From the way her breasts stood out, she had taken, I thought cattily, the precaution of wearing a good bra. On her feet were golden sandals. Amanda had changed to a ruby red robe of the hostess-gown sort.

Pancho, after a couple of arrogant sniffs, curled up with his long head resting on his front paws. He closed his eyes but his ears remained at half-mast, lest he miss something.

Lieutenant Tisbury got himself a straight and sturdy chair. He placed it near Sergeant Gomez, with its back towards the two sofas. He straddled it. He had left his brown hat in the hall. His black hair was brushed back smooth and shining above his wide brown forehead.

"We're ready, Miss Willoz."

A sigh escaped Rosemary. She did not answer. The contrast of her pale lovely hair against Amanda's rich red crepe robe was dramatic, and Rosemary was certainly aware of it.

Amanda looked hard, determined, and cool.

"My sister has decided to say nothing, Lieutenant Tisbury."

Rosemary said, "I guess maybe I'd better not after all."

"But you've already said it," Tisbury said. "All you need do is repeat what you've already told us, Miss Willoz."

"But I'm not really sure."

"You said that your sister Mrs. Willoz was mistaken in the darkness for you. That you had a date out there to meet John McKim Forsythe."

Amanda said, "My sister must not say any more, Lieutenant Tisbury. Not until she has counsel."

At the card table Sergeant Gomez was putting down each word. His round, dark Spanish-American face was expressionless as a copper coin.

Tisbury said, "That's her privilege, Mrs. Dollahan. But you seem to forget that she has already talked."

"You took her unawares. My husband says she must not talk any more until our lawyer is present."

"Sure enough?" Tisbury said. But he wasn't stopped. "That's her privilege, ma'am. But it would make things easier for us if she would just say over again what she has already said, for the benefit of the record. After all, we've got other very conclusive proof."

"My sister Rosemary never left the house," Amanda said, quite as if the police detective had not spoken. "We do not want her to talk any more now, because we understand that any statement she makes can be used against her."

Lucius Brady said, "May I offer a suggestion, Lieutenant?" Tisbury nodded, though somewhat suspiciously, for, like myself, he obviously distrusted the city slicker. "May I say that if Miss Willoz can prove she was in the house at the time her sister was shot . . ."

"Oh, of course I can," Rosemary said, sitting up, and smiling that smile. "Of course. Sally knows I was in the house at that time. So does Amanda. And you, Jean you saw me as you went downstairs after you had been with Sally."

That was a good while earlier, I thought.

Tisbury said, "That can wait, Miss Willoz. Mrs. Dollahan, there is no need at all for your sister to talk any more until she is settled in her mind." The sly fox, I thought. "Would you mind repeating your theory as to why Mrs. Willoz was coming back to this house, Mrs. Dollahan, ma'am?"

"It was merely a theory. We do not know exactly why."

The detective let this pass.

"She lived all alone, you said?"

"She kept one maid. Her maid is a sister of our cook. We have a couple, as I explained, and the three of them went to Waco yesterday afternoon to some sort of family gathering. They will not return until tomorrow."

"Who knew this?"

"Why, all the family, I presume. What difference does it make?"

"It makes a lot, ma'am. If her maid had been in her house last night we might know why she came back here." Nobody spoke, and Tisbury said, "She walked, we now know, because Mr. Brady had taken her car."

"She walked because she liked to walk," Rosemary said.

"She frequently walked here," Amanda said. "The distance is hardly more than three blocks."

"But she wore very high heels?"

"Juliana always wore high heels."

"On a rainy night? In the dark? And no sidewalks part of the way?"

Amanda said, "Juliana had no fear. And it was not raining at the time she came back here, was it? I understand the rain came after the . . . the body was found?"

"That's right," Tisbury said. His arms rested on the back of the chair. Their reticences bounced off him as if his shiny brown skin were granite. "Still, I would think a lady in her evening clothes would hesitate, ma'am, at that hour of the night, and with all the crime that goes on nowadays. She must have had a strong reason for walking back here alone in the dark."

"If you had known my sister Juliana you would know that she had a habit of doing things on the spur of the moment. She was impulsive. She evidently got a sudden notion that she wanted to see me. Us, I should say. It couldn't wait, so over she came. She had no phone, you know. She bought that house not long ago, and so far has not been able to get a telephone."

"Sure enough?" Tisbury said. It was indifferent. Not being able to get a phone was an old postwar story. He spoke abruptly to Rosemary. "Miss Willoz, ma'am, we took the gun that killed your sister off of young Forsythe. We found the shell it kicked out, outside the house. Only one shot had been fired. The gun had been fired so recently that it still gave off the smell of cordite. Anything you can tell us . . ."

"She is not going to tell you anything," Amanda said.

"You make it hard, Mrs. Dollahan, ma'am," Tisbury said reproachfully. "You run up big bills for the taxpayers."

"I'll talk," Rosemary said. She sat up straight and looked brave. She dabbed her eyes with a handkerchief. "I was to meet Kim, by the creek. I was to give him something." She dabbed again at her tears. "We had been having an affair, you see, and I . . . I promised . . ."

"Really, darling," Amanda said. "It is not necessary to tell these men things like that."

"I'll never have any peace till I do. My poor sister is dead because I was so foolish as to . . . to promise to meet Kim by the creek. I made a date. He was to wait in the street and I was to walk along the path by the creek and when we met I had promised to give him . . . something."This time she was not interrupted, but she herself digressed. Amanda looked too annoyed to trust herself to speak. "I felt awfully unhappy. We had had a nice party. But I felt very depressed and as soon as we got home I went upstairs. I changed into these dark clothes and got ready to meet Kim where we had agreed. I waited till the time we were to meet, which was to be right after the last car left the place. The last to go was the Abbotts'. They left a little after one and then, just as I was about to start downstairs, the back stairs—I had opened my door, in fact—why, Sally Dollahan took the dog out. That little dog, there."

Everybody looked at Pancho, who lifted his head and looked back with great dignity.

"So I did not leave the house. You see, after Sally went out there was a commotion of some kind, so I stayed in my room."

"You are sure that Miss Dollahan went out at that time?"

"I guessed so. She had the dog, on a leash. Naturally, she did go out."

"She doesn't deny it, dear," Amanda said. "Please, Lieutenant Tisbury, my sister is talking while under great emotional stress. What she is saying is not important, but it will be misinterpreted and reflect on her reputation, which is another reason why she must have a lawyer. What she called an affair is not an affair, in the usual sense, at all. The young man may be guilty of killing my sister. I do not know that, of course. But he is in my husband's employ and we don't want to injure him, either. Anything my sister says at this time confuses the issue. She is upset. It will do her harm and proves nothing. Besides, I have a confession to make. I have been holding back some evidence."

An expression of boredom, which had been fogging Tisbury's black eyes, vanished.

"I know why my sister came back."

"Sure enough?" Tisbury said, and this time it meant something.

"She came back because we had quarreled."

Ah, now we were getting places. The quarrel, the tense voices, the disturbed Juliana, the cold and angry Amanda. You're such a fool, Amanda had said. Oh, Sister, Juliana had cried. Please, I want you to approve, dear. Well, I don't, and I never shall, Amanda had said. Juliana had said it made her so happy—happy, Amanda had said, and the word was cold and harsh. The quarrel had ended for me with Amanda's forbidding Juliana to do something. What?

Amanda said, "We have always made it our rule never to go to sleep without at least trying to patch up any hard words we may have had. Usually the quarrels are my fault. I am the oldest sister, and I have always bossed the others, you might say. I am very dogmatic, but the girls never seemed to mind, and usually they have listened to me." Rosemary pressed Amanda's hand and gave her a loving glance. "Juliana had a very sweet nature. It was exceptional for her to stand up to me at all. Tonight, when she did do so, I'm afraid I wasn't very pleasant. Indeed, I was so harsh that I gave myself a headache, and therefore I went up to bed before our special guests, Mr. and Mrs. Abbott, had gone. Juliana went away while still angry and I'm certain that she came back simply to patch things up in our usual before-we-slept fashion."

"Why didn't she phone?"

"She has no telephone. I told you that."

Tisbury said, "You said you'd been withholding evidence, Mrs. Dollahan?"

"I'm telling it to you now."

"But you told us all this before, ma'am. Or approximately the same thing."

"I didn't tell you what we quarreled about, Lieutenant."

Tisbury nodded. "Well, what did you quarrel about, ma'am?"

Amanda glanced at Brady and back again to Tisbury.

"A string of black pearls."

"Black pearls?" The detective looked baffled. "Didn't know there was such a thing as a black pearl."

"Well, there is, and a good matched string can be very expensive. I most certainly would have made no objection if my sister could have afforded the pearls. She asked my advice. She was going to buy them as an investment. I told her not to. They would cost her three hundred thousand dollars which is more than her entire capital. She said that she could sell them again and double her money in a few months, but I said it was too risky. She asked my advice. I gave it. And then she refused to take it."

"Why, ma'am?"

"I don't know. I simply cannot understand why she was so very stubborn, especially when her suggestion didn't even make good sense."

Tisbury turned on Brady. His eyes gleamed.

"You were going to sell the deceased those black pearls?"

"My dear fellow! The matter had barely come up. She spoke about wanting to invest some money, and I mentioned the pearls."

"You told her the price?"

"Only approximately. After all, you don't buy and sell that sort of thing over the bargain counter. Mrs. Willoz wanted an investment, and I said the best thing we had at that moment was a string of perfect black pearls, and that I would write immediately and make certain of the exact sum they could be had for. The approximate price was three hundred thousand dollars. Which is what I mentioned to Mrs. Willoz. Tentatively. They were, you understand, part of an estate."

Tisbury didn't understand exactly. He gave Brady another hard look. "Go on, ma'am."

"You must understand, Lieutenant, that Mr. Brady is an old friend. I have often invested in jewels, on his advice, and I've done very well in them. The pearls are no doubt an excellent investment. Mr. Brady would not have said so, were they not. What I objected to, and a thing that doubtless Mr. Brady did not know, is that my sister's entire capital amounts to very little more than the price of those pearls. To sell her stocks and bonds, in order to speculate in pearls, would be insane."

"Sure enough," Tisbury said. He could make that expression mean anything. "Thank you, ma'am. Now, Miss Willoz, you went upstairs and changed, in order to go out and meet this guy with something dark on instead of your white dress . . ."

"Lieutenant Tisbury!" Amanda cut in. "You must listen to me! I let Juliana go away angry. I was angry, I mean. She was not angry but distressed. She had the disposition of an angel. A quarrel like that would torment her all night. And I might have known that she would come back."

"You couldn't know that I would take her car, Amanda," Brady said. "You could not know that she would walk back."

"I am to blame," Amanda said. "Lucius, I am to blame for Juliana's death. I had no right to let her go away upset."

Tisbury grabbed this chance to go back to Rosemary.

"Miss Willoz, ma'am, just how serious did you say was this affair you were having with young Forsythe?"

Amanda's voice cracked like a whip.

"Don't answer him, Rosemary!"

Patrick said, "May I ask a question, Lieutenant?"

"Why not?" Tisbury said. "Everybody else does."

"I'm curious about the motive for this murder," Patrick said. "I'm wondering how many people present thought that Mrs. Juliana Willoz would come into a great deal of money because of the death of Ulysses B. Green?"

9

THERE was one of those cold brittle silences. No clock ticked, because there was no such timepiece in this formal room. With a singular unity all eyes remained on Patrick Abbott. Even Lieutenant Tisbury's. He did manage a thin difficult curvature that might be called a smile, but his lips stayed tight, covering up his nice white teeth.

"If you're talking about the oil man Ulysses Green, just what do you mean?" And he added, "Might as well drag him in like everybody else, I reckon. We've already dragged in everything but the kitchen sink. I might ask who's conducting this inquiry, incidentally."

"You know Green?" Patrick asked.

"My home town is Big Spring. He's well known in West Texas."

Patrick grinned at Tisbury.

"Possibly I've handed you a very handsome clue, Lieutenant."

"Much obliged," Tisbury drawled.

"You're welcome."

Amanda said, "Mr. Green was my sister's divorced husband."

Tisbury took off his sarcastic smile.

"You mean, the sister that was murdered?"

Amanda winced, but said, with composure, "They had been divorced several years. They took no interest whatever in one another, after the divorce."

"I understand Green had been wanting her to marry him again." Patrick said,

If Tisbury had had ears like our Pancho you would have seen them prick up.

"What nonsense!" Amanda said.

"Why?"

"Juliana always told me everything. If she were planning to marry Mr. Green again she would have told me so."

Patrick said, "I didn't say that. I said I understood he wanted to remarry her. She struck me as a companionable woman. She could not have much liked living all alone, Mrs. Dollahan."

"For goodness' sake!" Amanda cried. "That was what caused the divorce. She was always alone. Ulysses Green was never home. That is, in whatever they called home at the moment. He dragged her all over Texas. The poor girl had no life at all. It's not likely she would want to go back to that."

"She wouldn't have had to. Green is said to have struck it very rich."

"Money wouldn't make any difference. Ulysses Green wasn't civilized. He liked living like a tramp."

"Irrelevant and immaterial, as the lawyers say," Tisbury said. "May I ask, Mr. Abbott, why you chose to introduce this information? At this time?"

"I thought you might like to establish a motive, Lieutenant."

"Motive? We've got a motive."

"You mean, you *think* you have. Mrs. Dollahan, was a woman mixed up in your sister's divorce?"

"Ridiculous!" Amanda said indignantly.

Tisbury cleared his throat.

"With your permission, Mr. Abbott, I will resume charge of the questioning."

Patrick grinned widely and said, "Granted, Lieutenant. I just happen to think it interesting to play around with the notion that if Green died rich, and Juliana Willoz was his beneficiary, and her two sisters were hers . . ."

"How dare you!" Amanda said.

"Whatever else, in shocking taste," Brady muttered.

Patrick said, "Like murder, Mr. Brady?"

"Really, Mr. Abbott," Brady snapped. "When you consider the circumstances . . . the natural grief . . ."

"Excuse me, Mr. Brady," Tisbury said. "What I object to is the time this irrelevant material takes. We have a motive, just as I said. Guy gets in a jam with one girl, wants another, bumps off number one . . . or tries to but shoots sister by mistake . . . and that's that."

"Has to be proved, Lieutenant," Patrick said cheerfully.

"We'll prove it!" Tisbury's black eyes snapped with anger. "Who's paying you to horn in on this case, Abbott?"

"Nobody. You requested my presence, Lieutenant. And I have a special reason to want justice done. This dog, while trying to do what he considered his duty, almost lost his life. I consider it my duty to finish what the dog started, since he can't talk."

"Thank God for that!" Tisbury said. "About all we need right now is for the dog to start talking, too."

He got off his chair suddenly and strode towards the door which opened into the hall between the living room and den. He went out and closed the door. Sergeant Gomez turned to stare after him, and Patrick, requesting for his cigarette a light he didn't need, crossed over to Brady and in passing dropped the flying red horse into Amanda Dollahan's lap.

With an expression of delighted relief Amanda picked it up and clipped it into the V of her ruby red robe. Brady's high brow wrinkled with a momentary bewilderment. Rosemary's head was again on her sister's shoulder, her eyes closed, so it seemed to me that she had missed seeing the return of the flying red horse.

Amanda said, in a friendly tone, "Iles feels so badly about your dog. Is it true that Ulysses Green is dead?"

"According to his doctor."

"But how? And when?"

"Something he ate. And last night some time, I believe. I wondered if he happened really to be rich."

Amanda said scornfully, "Like all his kind probably. Rich one day and poor the next."

"Sure, but if he died rich . . ."

"It would mean nothing to Juliana. Have meant, I should have said."

"He paid alimony?"

Sergeant Gomez was writing down what was said.

Amanda showed distaste. "He made a settlement, which was fair enough considering what he was worth at that time. This was invested in sound securities and government bonds and Juliana lived on the interest." She turned to Brady. "It was this money that she proposed to put into the black pearls, Lucius. She wasn't very practical, ever. That was why her suggesting it made me angry. Well, I was right enough, but that doesn't make me feel any better at this time. If I had dreamed what was to happen . . ."

"Darling, how could you have?" Rosemary asked.

"I'm so very sorry, too," Brady said. "I feel guilty. I should have consulted you, Amanda."

Lieutenant Tisbury returned.

"That will do, Mrs. Dollahan, ma'am. Also, Miss Willoz may go now. You'd better get some rest. And you, too, Mr. Brady. Keep in touch, Mr. Brady. I mean, if you leave your hotel, leave word at the desk where we can reach you. If we need to. That'll be all for now, though."

They went out, giving us little nods in passing, and Tisbury whirled on Patrick.

"Your timing's bad, fella. One more minute and I'd've had that girl's statement in black and white and the case would have been signed and sealed. Now, I start all over again. Forsythe isn't so young and innocent as you may think. He just happens to want the boss's daughter, who's also in line for a fat slice of his dough, probably. But he's mixed up with Rosemary Willoz, who's determined not to let him go." He said suddenly, "Sergeant, bring back Brady. I guess I'd better ask him a few routine questions right now."

Patrick said, "Mind if I sit in?"

"Not if you keep your trap shut."

"It's a deal, Lieutenant."

Brady came back, sat down where the women had been sitting, thus facing the police detective and took from his gold case another Egyptian cigarette.

"Tell us where you went after you left this house with Mrs. Willoz," Tisbury said.

Brady lit the cigarette and returned the gold lighter to his pocket. His dreamy eyes and his wide full-lipped mouth looked sad. His melodious voice was pitched in a low, convincing tone.

"There isn't much to tell, I'm afraid. I drove Mrs. Willoz home, in her own car, which she had suggested that I might use tomorrow morning. However, unless she wanted the car earlier, I was to pick her up about one o'clock for lunch. We took the usual route on leaving the house, following the street to the cross street, crossing the bridge, and turning back along the boulevard to the first light, then left and halfway up the block to Mrs. Willoz's house. I drove into the drive, opened the car door for her, took her key, and unlocked her front door. She had left a lamp on in the hall. I made a circuit of the house and she laughed at me for my caution. But her maid was away and I didn't like to think of her entering an empty house alone at night. I left lights on in her living room and her bedroom, said goodnight, and left her in the hall, closing the front door as I came out."

"How long were you in the house?"

"Five minutes at the most."

"Did you happen to notice the time?"

"Yes, we spoke of it. I left at five minutes to one."

"Did she say anything that would make you think she would return to Mrs. Dollahan's?"

"Of course not. I would have left her the car. Or driven her back, preferably."

"Was her behavior normal?"

"She seemed a little worried. She said she would tell me about it tomorrow. Said tonight she was going to take a sleeping capsule and go straight to bed."

"She didn't mention what had worried her?"

Brady hesitated. "She said she had quarreled with her sister. Mrs. Dollahan. They usually get along like a house afire and I daresay the tiff worried her more than it should have done."

"That tiff, as you call it, concerned those black pearls. I seem to keep thinking about black pearls, Mr. Brady, never having seen or heard of a black pearl up to now. Mrs. Dollahan felt that Mrs. Willoz could not afford these pearls, I believe."

"I am sorry I did not know that, Lieutenant."

"How come?"

Brady said sharply, "My dear sir, a transaction of that kind is of a strictly private nature. When Mrs. Willoz approached me about the pearls I most assuredly didn't run to Mrs. Dollahan to ask if she could afford them. I said I would make inquiry and find out if they were still available and let Mrs. Willoz know."

"You wrote a letter?"

"My plan was instead of writing to telephone. This morning, as soon as our shop opened, in New York."

"Just where did you say those pearls were, Mr. Brady?"

Squirming in spite of himself, Brady said, "In Ferrier's vaults, in New York City."

"And how did the subject happen to come up with Mrs. Willoz?"

"In the usual way. Mrs. Willoz wanted to buy some jewels, for investment. I spoke to her about the pearls. Her sister, Mrs. Dollahan, has frequently made a pretty penny in stones. So if Mrs. Willoz wanted to see what she could do with a good buy in black pearls, why not? Here's another thing, Lieutenant. Mrs. Dollahan is a regular customer. Therefore, you can be very sure that I would not make the mistake of giving Mrs. Willoz unsound advice on her investment. You can lose customers very quickly in my business. I didn't know, of course, that she didn't have money to play around with. Naturally, I'd no idea that she planned to put all her eggs in that one basket."

"If you had, you would have advised her against the pearls?"

"Certainly!"

Tisbury shrugged.

"Personally I can't see it. Give me the horses any day. Well, what happened after you left Mrs. Willoz?"

"I returned to the car, backed out of the drive, and drove to my hotel. Or rather, to the Baker Garage, where I left the car."

"You didn't see Mrs. Willoz after she . . . or rather you . . . closed her front door, then?"

"In point of fact, I did. Briefly. She opened the door just as I got back into the street from the drive, and waved."

"And then she closed the door again?"

"I don't know," Brady said slowly. "I drove on past her house and came around the block back to the boulevard and didn't see her again. The car is a convertible with a deep hood. You don't have too clear a rear view, I'm afraid. Why?"

"Routine question. Was Mrs. Willoz jealous of her sister?"

There was another eloquent moment of silence.

Then Brady said, "What do you mean?"

"Of Mrs. Dollahan, I mean."

"Oh. Oh, no. They seemed the best of friends. I was a little surprised when Mrs. Willoz said they had had words, but that happens in the best families, as you know. I think Mrs. Willoz really revered her sister. She admired very much Mrs. Dollahan's chic, and her business acumen. She frequently said that Amanda was the real success of the family. She loved the younger sister dearly. Either can—could always—forgive Rosemary anything."

"Anybody see you put the car in the Baker garage, Mr. Brady?"

"Rather. They give you a check, you know, with the exact time punched on it."

"Better give it to me," Tisbury said.

Brady took out a crocodile billfold with gold corners and from it gave the police detective the garage check.

"1:15 A.M.," Tisbury said. "This check is part of your alibi, Mr. Brady. What did you do after you left the car?"

"I walked around to the side entrance of the hotel and went into the lobby. I collected the key at the desk, and a telegram from my firm in New York, and then I took the lift upstairs."

"Lift?"

"Elevator. The boy knows me and will remember my coming in, I think. I sat down in my room to write a letter to Ferrier's about the black pearl necklace."

"So you wrote a letter?"

It was a neat finesse, planned no doubt merely to remind Brady that he had mentioned telephoning a few minutes ago.

"No, I did not. By then a letter seemed futile, since I could telephone for the information I wanted within a few hours."

"Maybe you wanted to wait till the banks opened, so you could check on your client's ability to pay?"

"I beg your pardon!"

"Forget it," Tisbury said. "What happened then?"

Brady looked a little apologetic.

"Well, it doesn't make sense, but I went out and ate a middle of the night breakfast at the B & B cafe. After all the fancy fare we'd been indulging in all evening, I suddenly longed for something like their sausage and eggs."

Tisbury relaxed. It was the first thing Brady had said which in his opinion really made sense.

"Sure enough," he said. "And then what?"

"I returned to my room. I had just turned in when your men called for me."

"Thank you, Mr. Brady. I suppose you used the elevator when you went out to the B & B cafe?"

"I walked down. My room is on the third floor. I used the elevator on my return."

"I reckon that's all at present." Then Tisbury looked at Patrick, gleamed, and said, "Like to ask any questions, Mr. Abbott?"

Brady gave Tisbury a puzzled look, and Patrick another, as Patrick said, "Thank you, Lieutenant. Mr. Brady, tell me, what were your intentions towards Juliana Willoz?"

For the flick of an instant Brady was ill at ease, and then he said, "Your question is in the most execrable taste!"

"Right," Patrick said. "That's all, Lieutenant Tisbury."

10

"THIS is terrible!" Amanda Dollahan said, just before we again left her house, this time at three-forty in the morning.

"It's a hell of a note!" Iles Dollahan growled.

"It's shocking," asserted Lucius Brady.

Lieutenant Tisbury said, "It's routine. Sorry to bother you folks, but you have to follow a certain routine in a case of murder."

"It's late," Patrick said. "Give you a lift downtown, Brady?"

Amanda said, "Stay for a cup of coffee, won't you, Lucius?"

Brady accepted so quickly that I felt he used the invitation to avoid us. Iles asked us to remain, but Amanda did not want us and did not second his invitation. Also Patrick was anxious to be off.

Amanda had come downstairs a few minutes after going up with Rosemary. The younger sister had responded at once, Amanda said, to a sleeping pill, but she herself was in no mood for sleep. She was still in her red robe, but not now wearing the flying ruby horse Patrick had returned to her.

She had voiced, in her studied contralto, on coming back, anxiety about her husband, about Sally Dollahan, who was mysteriously absent, and about Kim Forsythe, whom the police were holding for questioning. Her remarks virtually condemned the boy.

"These young men!" she said. "The war made killers of so many. They crave excitement. For certain types the war was a glorious experience. It will take a lifetime to straighten out the troubles caused by the war."

Lieutenant Tisbury was polite, but he refused to be drawn into any chitchat. When we left the house his shiny black eyes followed us as though he could hardly resist pursuit.

"He was glad to be rid of you, Pat. You made him uncomfortable."

"He makes me uncomfortable too, Jeanie."

"Why?"

"I was virtually on the scene of the crime. Tisbury makes me feel that I slipped badly."

We had arrived on the bridge beside the waterfall.

"Now where?"

"First I want to find out how much territory got that shower." The moon was shining again. The air was sweet after the rain, and in the moonlight the leaves glistened from their wetting, and the pavement was damp, with little puddles in the uneven places which gleamed blackly before our headlights.

We turned left on Turtle Creek Boulevard and kept on the boulevard till it wound through a small green park and came out on the curving thoroughfare by which I had entered Dallas less than twelve hours ago. It was called Harry Hines Boulevard. There we turned left. One block and a half on and we were out of the areas dampened by the shower. The pavement was dry. Dust made the leaves of the street-side shrubbery dull and drab-looking.

Patrick stopped and turned and headed back the way we had come. He checked the distance on the speedometer.

"Kim could have done the murder and have been either in or out of the area where it rained before he took the cab. His having been rained on means virtually nothing."

"Iles had the gun."

"Yes. If that's the murder weapon, it was left somewhere on the Dollahan place."

"That doesn't make sense, Pat. Why would he leave the murder gun where Iles could pick it up? And why would Iles do it?"

Patrick was turning back through the little park.

"Nothing makes sense, so far, Jean."

"Specially what we are doing now. I'm hungry, like Lucius Brady was when he got back to the hotel."

"Okay. First, I got from Tisbury the name of a kennel near here which stays open all night. We've got to park this pooch."

Pancho knew what was up. He pressed his warm smooth body closer against my thigh.

"After all he did, Pat! Reporting the murder, and all!"

"He still can't talk. And the dog-catcher at the hotel looked mild, but also firm."

The kennel was on Lemmon Avenue. We left the heartbroken dog, and cut back to Harry Hines Boulevard by way of Lucas Street. An old car followed behind us, a car which dated back to the days before headlights were set in the fenders. It looked like a face with eyes set too close to the bridge of the nose.

Arriving at the boulevard, Patrick pulled up for a look at the view. The midtown section rose up like a city in a dream.

"Gosh!"

"I told you it was pretty special, Pat."

"There ought to be a special name for it."

"There is, dear. They call it Dallas."

"Hey?"

"And it's full of places to eat. I'm starved. And I'm worried. I want to go back to the hotel, after we eat, and be comfortable and unbothered. I'm worried, and I don't know why exactly. Oh, yes, I do. I'm worried about those kids."

"So am I. You shall be fed, my darling, but first we're driving out to Love Field."

"*Where?*"

"Don't be alarmed. It's the Dallas airport. I want to ask a question or two."

As we moved into and along the boulevard the narrow-eyed car showed up behind us again. We were moving at around the legal thirty miles an hour. The car pottered at the same speed.

"Pat, you aren't flying out to Odessa?"

"I won't need to. When Tisbury left us—that time I gave Amanda her horse back—he called the police department to check up on Ulysses B. Green."

"How do you know?"

"Well, wouldn't you have? If you were a policeman?"

"Yes. You don't think Kim did the murder, do you, Pat?"

"No."

"Even if the police do think so, they have to prove it."

"Yes. But it's a lot better to prove that he didn't do it, dear. And the best way to do that is to prove who did do it."

"Have you any idea?"

"I've got a swell idea. Only, it doesn't click. Keep an eye on that old car behind us, Jeanie. We should turn right at the next corner for Love Field, and I'm going to roam around a bit to see if it's tailing us."

He slowed, and made a right turning. The little car followed. Patrick stepped on the gas hard and whizzed right around the next corner. The car tailed us but was losing ground. Patrick turned right again fast. Back on the boulevard he was still driving fast. He drove two blocks beyond the spot where we had turned right previously. The narrow-eyed car had not shown up, so he turned right again and maneuvered in the direction of the airport, taking it easy again.

"That was quick, Pat."

"Too quick. It was an old car, but it didn't have to lose us as easy as all that. Keep an eye peeled for it."

"Pat, just how did you happen to get a hunch about this Ulysses B. Green?"

"Curiosity. Juliana was in such a high mood all evening. It got on her sister's nerves. It apparently resulted in that quarrel with Amanda which you partly overheard. When Kim told us that Green wanted to marry her again, and had picked up a lot of new oil money lately, I got curious. I decided to telephone Green. I've been wondering what I would have said if he had been alive and able to talk, because it wasn't

Green's wanting to marry Juliana again which was making her so gay this evening."

"Then what was it?"

"Love is your department, babe."

"Pat, Juliana would love any man who paid her any special attention. She'd had very little attention in her life, if I'm any judge."

"Right. But Brady was courting her. He didn't show it openly, of course. He wouldn't. Maybe he just wanted to sell her the pearls. Could be. He's a mercenary devil, I bet. Juliana was out of this world. Her sisters knew something was up. I'm still inclined to think they didn't know exactly what it was. She was dying to tell everybody about it. You asked me to dance with her, you know, and if I had fished half a spot deeper while we were dancing—if you could call the walking you did with Juliana dancing—Juliana would have told me her whole secret. As it was, she told me enough to give me some insight into her plans."

"And you think she may have told Amanda?"

"No. I think they really quarreled because Juliana told Amanda that she was going to buy the black pearls. And I think after leaving the house and going home Juliana decided to come back and tell her what she wanted to tell everybody, all evening."

"Meaning?"

"That Green had died, leaving her a good deal of money. And maybe also that she was going to marry Brady."

"Pat, you don't know any of that. It's all guess work."

"Yep."

"How come?"

"Well, the money alone wouldn't make Juliana that happy. She was a congenial person. Yet she had to live alone. The marriage she had had with Green was broken up. Now he wanted to marry her again, but for some reason she had held off. Probably Amanda was against it. And then she fell for Brady. They all do. Even you put on trills and frills when he pays you attention, Jeanie."

"I don't!" I declared indignantly.

"You do! With Juliana, who never got much notice from anybody, who was always the rug under the other sisters' feet, who expected nothing, and who suspected no evil in any one, attention from Brady would be like a stiff drink to a teetotaler. And why would Brady go after Juliana? Money, honey! Therefore Juliana must have been coming into what they call real money even in Dallas."

"He's pretty bad, Pat."

"No. Just an over-developed business instinct, maybe. Amanda is afflicted the same way."

"Poor Juliana."

"She was the happiest of the lot, and the chances are she never knew what hit her."

"But she got the raw deal, always."

"I doubt if she knew that. She didn't have Amanda's smartness or Rosemary's sex appeal—"

"Is that what you call it?"

"Sure. It's old as time, of course. Rosemary's is what they call in the Bible the wisdom of the serpent. But remember, Juliana was not jealous, or critical, or mean. She took it for granted that life held not so much for her as for the others. And it certainly never occurred to either of her sisters that pleasant and romantic happenings were in store for Juliana. She was the homely sister, the dull one, the accommodating one. Amanda managed life well. She had success, the kind she wanted. Rosemary got what she wanted, too, in one way or another. And here suddenly was Juliana, clattery, dowdy Juliana, who looked older than her older sister Amanda, who always did the wrong thing, about to hit the jackpot. A fortune from Green, and, for a husband, Brady."

"But they didn't know that?"

"No. But Rosemary senses things, connives, plans. And Amanda thinks them through. They suspected the truth, certainly. Juliana clattered, and she didn't normally float around on a cloud without telling everybody why."

I said, "I'll admit Brady is fascinating, Pat."

"He knocks you women for a loop. He winds you around his neat, manicured fingers. Men like me and Iles and Kim detest the Brady type. But there he is, always present in some way or other, and always getting in where we can't make the grade."

"I can't see him marrying Juliana."

Patrick said, "Well, who would Brady marry? He has never been married, I understand. Why not? Because marriage would cramp his style. But suppose, along with a wife, he might get a good many millions. And a wife like Juliana would be fine. Uncomplicated. Good. Unsuspicious. Malleable. That's the kind he would probably settle for. Not the possessive kind, like Rosemary, or the managing kind, like Amanda. Juliana would be his cup of tea. And he'd do something about her. He'd put her in the hands of great dressmakers and coiffeurs. He'd choose her clothes and her jewels. He'd make her chic. And she would adore it all and do just as she was told."

"It seems far-fetched . . ."

"Not at all. Juliana was used to doing what she was told. She would worship a husband like Brady. She would never realize that he was merely ambitious, selfish, vain and mercenary."

"Then the black pearls . . ."

"Were possibly to have been for her own use. A distinctive necklace which would give her chic, along with being a good investment. If he didn't know that Juliana was to come into money . . ."

"As you don't, Patrick!"

". . . he would have offered the pearls first to Amanda, who invested in jewels, I suspect. Not in little ordinary fifteen-thousand-dollar items like her ruby clips. Those were for wearing, not for investment. I don't know anything about what Amanda buys, of course . . ."

"Of course you don't."

". . . but I'm certain she is a good customer and that Brady would not have offered the pearls first to Juliana unless she was coming into more money than she already possessed. Therefore he knew that Green was dead. He knew that Juliana was to inherit. She told him and he told her not to tell anyone else and asked her to marry him and swore her to keep it quiet. And that was pretty tough on good, open-hearted, talkative Juliana."

"Pat, I never heard the like! Usually it's me whose imagination goes haywire."

"Right."

"What you have been saying is strictly hooey. And I'm simply starving."

"Right."

Patrick stopped, took his bearings, and drove on.

"Surely she told you something? A little?" I asked.

"She told me when we danced that she was in love and that it was just like a story in a book. She said she had been married when she was twenty to a man who was thirty years older than she was, and that it was a happy marriage but that she had never been crazy about him, as she was about somebody now. That means that Green was pretty old when he died. Juliana said that she had always wanted children and if she married again, she wanted a family. After that I kept an eye open and I saw her holding hands with Brady."

"Don't you suppose the others saw it?"

"Maybe. But they didn't know how much it all meant. Brady meant to marry her. I'm sure of it."

I said, "If what you think was true, the money will probably go to her sisters. . . . Pat, that looks like the car which was tailing us."

It could have been just another little car of the same vintage. It was buzzing along now, in a great hurry. We rolled along behind it and when it parked just outside the entrance to the airport Patrick rolled in close by. Then both its doors flew open. Sally Dollahan jumped out of one of them and out of the other Kim Forsythe. Kim flung on a topcoat as he ran. In the glare of white light which surrounds all airports at night they met in front of the old car in a heart-warming clinch.

"Wow!" I said.

An air liner was warming up around the edge of the field. Others stood gleaming, while mechanics worked them over. One, its motors humming, was loading passengers just inside the gates.

Kim gave Sally another long kiss. She finally gave him a little push and he dashed off to the waiting plane. He was the last aboard. He flapped a farewell wave as the door shut him inside. With a last, lonely flap of her own hand, Sally, drooping a little, walked around the old car and got in. She lit a cigarette slowly, and then started the noisy motor and drove off.

"It couldn't've been they who followed us, Pat."

"If so, I wonder why. Want to come inside with me?"

We entered the terminal building and Patrick went to a ticket window. The agent was very co-operative. He gave Patrick the hours planes left for Odessa or Midland, either directly or with a change here or there. Yes, Mrs. Juliana Willoz had reservations on the seven o'clock plane. Mrs. Willoz and sister. Which sister? She had not said.

"Thank you," Patrick said. He asked for timetables covering all flights in West Texas and the agent got them without questioning. Patrick thanked him again, and the agent thanked Patrick. On the bulletin board an attendant was erasing the flight Kim Forsythe had taken. It also included Midland among its stops. By this time my geography was good enough to realize that Odessa and Midland were not far apart, for Texas.

11

Patrick put the car in the Adolphus Garage, took the claim check, and we walked out on Commerce Street. In the emptiness of the hour the street looked narrow and cavernous on account of the tall buildings. The street itself was shining clean and the wind blew. There was almost no traffic, so that a car stopping for the blinker where Akard Street jogged across Commerce, and then moving on, caught attention. The car was an old cabriolet, such as Sally Dollahan had been driving at the airport.

High, high and now straight above us flew the Magnolia Building's flying red horse. Touched perhaps by the beginning of the dawn, which was not yet discernible at street level, it looked fresh and rosy with life as it turned on its pedestal.

We walked around the corner to the B & B cafe, where we each drank a tumbler of fresh orange juice, and had a stack of wheatcakes, coffee, and a lot of crisp bacon. When we returned to the hotel there was a telegram in our box and the clerk reported a series of telephone calls.

"Man or woman?"

"The operator did not say, sir."

"Any messages?"

"No, sir. No name was left at any time. If the party calls again want it put through?" The clerk glanced I at the clock.

"Not at this hour," I said. The clerk smiled, Patrick moved his eyebrows eloquently, and we took the elevator upstairs.

As we entered our suite the telephone rang. Patrick took it.

"Yes? . . . Oh, hello, Lieutenant . . . Yes, they said at the desk someone had kept calling . . . Had to find that kennel you told me about for the dog . . . No, just took a ride and then dropped in at the B & B for something to eat . . . Sorry, but I don't know a thing . . . What the devil would I work against the police for? My client? But I told you that my client is our dog. . . . Sure. . . . So long!"

"Now what?" I asked, as Patrick hung up.

He was smiling. "They've lost Kim Forsythe."

"Good. I'm glad you didn't give him away."

"Why should I? They're also looking for Sally Dollahan. She slipped out of the house while they were talking to the other suspects and nobody knows where she is. The police thought at first that Sally and Kim might have gone in Dollahan's plane, but the plane hasn't been taken."

"I thought I saw her just after we put the car in."

"You did see her," Patrick said. He chuckled aloud. "Maybe she's riding around in that old crate for the fun of it. Or maybe she was tailing us. I think that explains why she tailed us when we were near the airport, though. She was taking Kim to the plane and she wanted to make sure we didn't know what she was up to, so she jockeyed around us till the last minute. She may have seen us after Kim left. I'm sure she didn't just before he boarded the plane, considering that clinch under the bright lights." Patrick laughed out loud. "Tisbury said that one of their best men was on Kim's trail, but the boy gave him the slip. Well, shut-eye for me, baby."

And about time. It was five-thirty in the morning, and me with a big shopping day ahead, I hoped. And with Kim off the scene at the moment, and Sally too, I suddenly felt there was nothing to worry about. Iles Dollahan could work out his own problems, and I didn't really care what happened to those others, I decided, as I was slipping off to sleep.

Suddenly I woke. I didn't know why at first. Then I heard the sound of a tiny click, so slight that it might have been an insect flicking against a parchment shade. It took my attention toward the door from the sitting room. Enough light was coming in between the louvers so that I could see plainly a shadowy figure and a darkly shining pistol.

The click had been the releasing of the safety catch on the gun.

Shivers ran over me. I glanced at Patrick. He was lying perfectly still. Sound asleep, I thought. Oh, the big so-and-so! The things he got us into!

The figure took another step. Because of a wisp of light I saw that it was Sally Dollahan.

Patrick drawled abruptly, "Go easy with that six-shooter, Sally. I never did like guns."

Sally said flatly, "Don't make a fuss, now."

I gasped. Now I knew how scared I was. Shivers ran up and down my back as Patrick calmly sat up, turned on the lamp, and reached for a cigarette.

Sally Dollahan, still standing near the door, the gun gripped in her right hand, was entirely under control. She was just as calm as Patrick. She appeared to consider the matter, then she calmly put the safety catch on again and, refusing a chair, stood there tall and easy. Her face was as hard and clean-cut as a cameo.

"How did you get in?" Patrick asked, just as easily.

"Through the door. You forgot to lock it."

"Doesn't matter. No doubt you would have come in through the transom in a pinch. A determined lass like you."

"Why not? When I decide to do a thing I do it."

"Can't say the same for myself," Patrick said.

I said, "Sally, what do you want?"

Without answering Sally started tossing the automatic back and forth in her hands, as a child does a ball. It gave me gooseflesh. But not wanting to have her know I was the only frightened one present, I sat up myself, reached for the cigarettes, and took one. I waved the package at Sally, who shook her head, and went on flipping that gruesome gun around. As I gave myself a light my hand was shaking. I hoped they didn't notice.

"How did you get into the hotel?" Patrick asked.

"The usual way. Walked in. Registered. I was lucky and got a room on the floor just below yours, so I had only one flight to walk up."

"You registered as Sally Dollahan, of course?"

"As Mary Smith," Sally said. "I borrowed an overnight case from a friend named Marian Sullivan, which meant there had to be the initials M. S., so I signed in as Mary Smith."

"Very original," Patrick said.

"I think so too," Sally said, in the same mocking tone. Her eyes were shining. They looked bright green, like wonderful jewels in her small attractive face. Gone entirely was the worried and hysterical Sally who had been in a tizzy over our dog Pancho. Gone also was a Sally more self-contained, but slightly touched with bravado, who had talked to me, in her room, about the complications in her home and love life.

There was a reason, of course. She looked out of this world and it was because she was happy. This Sally, this attractive idiot playing jackstones with that deadly gun, was now sure of her man, and *so what* with everything and everybody else.

Patrick said, "So you borrowed a suitcase, registered here, then came up to call. Why didn't you phone first?"

"I thought the police might be checking your calls."

"Very likely," Patrick said. "You're a smart girl, Sally. Now put down that trinket and tell us just why you're here."

"You know why I came. You saw Kim take that plane. I'm here because I've got to make you promise that you won't tell where we went. I am perfectly capable of keeping you here at the point of this gun until Kim returns."

"Since we don't know where he went, it's easy not to tell, Sally."

I said, "If it's any comfort, the police have already called to ask about Kim and Patrick told them he knew nothing about him. I told Pat I was glad he didn't give him away. But if you don't get rid of that . . . that awful thing . . ."

"This?" Sally said, caressing the gun. "What's awful about it?"

"Plenty, if it goes well. This hotel even sends a house detective to collect a dog. We'll all be on the street if there's a gunshot. This is the second time you Dollahans have been up here pointing guns. You ought to go back to West Texas, or wherever people behave like you do, if that's the way you act."

"Well, if that's how you feel," Sally said, "I'll put it in my bag." She was wearing a dark green suit, and a brown leather handbag over her shoulder that would have been capacious enough even for Kim's forty-five. This pistol was of smaller calibre, a thirty-two or even less. "But before I do," she said, tossing the thing back and forth again, "I have to know what you were up to at the airport."

"Why did we have to be up to anything?" Patrick asked.

"You were spying on us," Sally said.

"Nothing of the kind. We noticed that you kept behind us, and I did a few turns and twists to get rid of you. We didn't know who you were until we caught up at the airport. You were enjoying yourself there, too."

Sally smiled and her eyes looked like pale emeralds.

Her behavior took a turn towards the normal.

"I sneaked out and borrowed that old crate and then I got in touch with Kim. We shoved off for the airport so that he . . . but never mind that part. Kim will be back all right. We thought you were tailing us. Maybe you were. So we had time to spare and we tailed you. It was fun to follow around after you for a block or two, just to pretend we were following you, but I had trouble with the car then and Kim almost missed the plane." She opened her bag and dropped the gun in. "Sorry about the gun. It's not loaded. I thought maybe you'd be difficult, so naturally I came prepared."

"Guns can get you into plenty of trouble, even when they're not loaded."

"That depends," Sally said. "It *was* a promise, wasn't it? I mean, about not telling that Kim took that plane?"

"Cross my heart, Sally."

"I'm going now."

"Good night," I said.

"If you don't mind," Patrick said, yawning, "will you put the night lock on the hall door as you go out, Sally?"

I said, as the hall door closed, and Patrick turned off the light, "Too many extreme individualists in this case, darling."

"Just Texans on a rampage, Jean."

I would never sleep now, I decided, but when startled suddenly by the telephone, I reached for it and at the same time looked at the clock, I had been sleeping almost two hours.

"Hello?" Patrick said on the phone.

I stared at his bed. It was empty. He was answering from the sitting room phone.

"Hello, Pat? This is Rosemary."

"Oh, hello, Rosemary. I had your telegram."

"Oh? I'm glad. I've been so frightfully worried it almost made me ill. I've just got to see you, Pat."

"Okay. When?"

"How about lunch?"

"Lunch? Fine, if you don't mind going on worrying till then. At what time, and where?"

"Twelve," Rosemary said. "That's early, but there won't be such a crowd. You meet me at Mario's, will you, Pat? There's wonderful food and it's not in the center of town and also it's a nice place so our being there won't look queer, if anybody does happen to see us. Besides, it's famous for the good food."

"All right. Where are you calling from?"

"Oh, I left the house and I'm phoning from a pay phone."

"Any trouble getting away?"

"Why, no, Pat. The police wouldn't suspect *me.*"

"I should hope not," Patrick purred.

Rosemary said, "I hope you didn't tell Jean about that telegram, Pat?"

"Of course not."

"She's awfully sweet, Pat. But I never do trust women, for some reason. I never tell a woman a single thing, except of course Amanda, and I don't tell her everything. She doesn't know I'm getting in touch with you, Pat."

"That's good. What's on your mind, Rosemary?"

"Oh, I daren't tell you on the phone. I mustn't. I've been so very foolish. Pat, honey . . . you won't tell your wife?"

"Certainly not . . . dear."

With difficulty I restrained a snort, which would have been fatal.

"You're sweet, honey. You're perfectly sweet. I have something . . . something I must talk to you about. I don't know what to do. They say that the police nowadays can find out anything. They say they can collect the ashes and read an entire letter. They pretend they have lost all interest and all the time they keep prying till sooner or later some gadget or other tells them what they are after. It's awful. Oh, I don't dare be dragged into this murder. I'm sorry for Juliana and all, but Amanda is right about scandal. That kind of thing is simply sordid."

"Can't you tell me what's worrying you, dear?" Patrick said.

"No, darling. Not on the phone. Mario's, then."

"Deposit five cents, please," an operator said.

"It's not necessary," Rosemary said coldly. She added softly, "See you at noon, darling."

Rosemary's receiver clicked. Patrick said, "You can hang up now, Jeanie-sugar-honey-pie."

He was grinning from ear to ear when I stalked out into the sitting room, all set to speak my piece. There he sat, in his pajamas and dressing gown, and beside him was a coffee service, but no more coffee.

"How long have you been up, Pat?"

"Since seven. I had a date with Iles at seven, remember. He didn't show."

"He's probably out gunning. What does that Rosemary want?"

"You know as much as I do . . . honey lamb."

"Honestly!" I snorted that snort at last. "The things a detective's wife has to swallow!"

Patrick shouted with laughter. Then he grabbed me and kissed me and rubbed his cheek against mine.

"You need to shave," I said coldly.

"Good idea," he said. He seemed in high spirits, and in spite of trying to use common sense I felt very jealous of Rosemary. It's all right to think and say such girls are out of date and all, but they score every time. And I was cross because Patrick had held out on me. I had seen him take the telegram at the desk, but what with one thing or another it had gone out of my mind. "I'll shave and shower and you order up breakfast. The usual for me," Patrick said.

I reminded him that we had breakfasted three hours ago and that he had just consumed a pot of coffee and was lunching early with the fair Rosemary, but he stood his ground as usual and went off to shave and shower only after I had called room service and given the order.

The shower was going when the phone rang again.

"Jean? This is . . . Mary Smith."

"Oh, hello . . . Mary."

"I've got to see you, Jean. But not until around lunch. I'm keeping under cover till lunch. Is lunch okay?"

"Fine," I said "Could you make it early? Say noon? And how about Mario's? instead of Neiman's?"

"Mario's is fine," Sally said. "Swell place to eat and sort of out of the way. And anyhow by that time my name won't be Smith."

"Good-bye for now, Smith."

Sally's gay laughter rippled over the phone and I laughed with her. Specially when thinking how Patrick and Rosemary would look when they saw Sally Dollahan and me walking in on them at Mario's.

12

PATRICK had shaved and showered and dressed in gray flannels and I had showered and done my hair and was all ready except for putting on my suit when breakfast arrived and I sat down to it, with good appetite too, in my white robe. At that moment the phone rang again. It was Amanda Dollahan, downstairs, and she asked to come up. Patrick said to come ahead and I said something to Pat, as I swallowed my orange-juice, about living in a constant procession of Dollahans.

Amanda wore a black suit with a white blouse. Her flying red horses were together at her throat. Her white heart-shaped face was a little haggard, but there was no relaxation of her chic.

She apologized for coming while we breakfasted. I said we were doing so much breakfasting this morning that it was practically impossible to arrive when we weren't. This perplexed but did not divert her. Amanda had come for a purpose, and she bade us go right along and eat while she told us what it was.

"I'm so worried about Iles," she said. "He's gone."

Iles gone? Inside myself, I sort of chuckled as I thought he had probably registered at this hotel, calling himself John Smith.

"Sally has gone, too. But I'm not worried about Sally. She is not suspected of any part in the murder of my sister. So it's different with her. But Iles has vanished in thin air and heaven only knows what has happened to him. I tried to get hold of Kim Forsythe, but he isn't in his room. I have not notified the police. I dare not."

"Iles had something on his mind," Patrick said.

"Yes. That was business. Though he didn't tell me exactly what. And it had nothing to do with any of the awfulness, last night."

"I see."

"There is something else. Lieutenant Tisbury has told me that my sister's former husband just died out in Odessa and had willed her a great deal of money. She had been notified, too. I'm simply horrified."

"Why?"

"Because I was so stern with her about those silly pearls. My goodness, had I known she was coming into a fortune I most certainly would not have talked to her as I did. But I don't understand it. I mean, why didn't she tell me?"

"Maybe some lawyer told her not to?"

"I thought of that. But that isn't enough, with Juliana. She always talked, regardless. I phoned Lucius—Lucius Brady—after the lieutenant told me about the money, and he was simply stunned. Juliana hadn't breathed a word to him about it, not a word. I was wondering if she said anything to you? She was greatly taken with you, Mr. Abbott. You were so very kind to her, last night."

We were back on a formal level. Mrs. Dollahan and Mr. and Mrs. Abbott.

"She seemed excited," Patrick said. "I did not know her well enough to know whether she was always like that or not, Mrs. Dollahan."

Amanda said, slightly off her even keel for half a moment, "I just can't understand it. She always told me every little thing. And Rosemary, too. She was always talking, always telling us—and others, too—every little thing." With one of her meticulously white-gloved hands she took out a handkerchief and touched the eyelashes of her handsome black eyes. "We kept many of our own secrets from her, I'm afraid. She talked so much. She would forget and tell, and therefore one always hesitated to entrust her with a confidence. But we loved her. Dearly. Yet, I simply can't understand her not telling one of us, or both, about this money. Ulysses Green recently had one of the most sensational strikes in all oil history. He may have left Juliana a vast fortune."

"What will happen to it then?"

"I don't know. I really don't know. If there are no other beneficiaries . . . and if Juliana made no will . . . and certainly if she had made a will she would have told us . . ."

"She didn't even hint about Green's death?" Patrick asked.

Amanda shook her head.

"She had known it only a few hours. Even so, it's phenomenal, in Juliana. I am sure she was on her way back to our house to tell me about it. She wanted me to know, because she realized that I had been grim about those wretched pearls because I thought she couldn't afford them. It's tragic. If she had only told me! If I had only known about all the money! Then everything would have been all right. She would have gone home happy and the accident would never have happened because she would have stayed home. It's too awful for words."

"Why did you think your sister was so excited last evening, Mrs. Dollahan?"

Amanda hesitated, frowned a tiny frown, then smoothed out her brow into its accustomed white perfection, and said, "This has nothing to do with anything. Please remember that, and do forget it immediately. She thought Lucius Brady had fallen in love with her." She bit at her lips, and then said, "That was really what started our quarrel. I spoke to her about it after we got to our house and told her she was being very silly. I didn't want her to cherish such an illusion and be hurt. Mr. Brady is a very sophisticated person. The things he says casually mean nothing to anybody with his point of view. But Juliana was so very childlike about affairs of the heart. She thought any man meant everything he said. She told me Lucius was in love with her, and I scolded her like a child."

I poured another cup of coffee for Patrick.

Amanda said, "She was in a state of girlish thrill and she was about to drive home with Lucius and it worried me. I was afraid she would give herself away, to him, and embarrass him, and then be miserable herself. She was going to be hurt anyway on account of the pearls. Or so I thought. Not knowing about the money which was coming to her, you see. So I told her frankly that if she tried to buy the pearls I would tell Lucius the truth about her money. He is perfectly honorable and he wouldn't think of letting her sink her last penny into a string of black pearls. Maybe they might go up in value, indeed if he says they will they will, because he's very clever in his business. But he wouldn't think of taking Juliana's every dollar for such an investment. It might be years and years before she could sell them and get her money back, you see. And of course he knew nothing about her finances. His deals have always been with me. Please remember that I acted entirely as I did because I hadn't an inkling about her inheritance."

Patrick said, "You are the eldest sister."

She nodded. "Yes. And I have an absurd sense of responsibility on account of it. Poor dear Juliana. She I was the best-hearted of us."

"Tell me more about yourself, Mrs. Dollahan."

She looked surprised. "But I came to talk about Iles."

"I know. But I'd like to know more about you, yourself. Frankly, I don't know what to suggest about Iles, but while you talk I'll think."

Amanda said, "Well, there is so little. I can't remember when I didn't have to work. I had to look after Juliana, and then Rosemary, because my mother went out as a seamstress or even as a cleaning woman by the day in order to bring in enough for us to live on. After school, later, I worked in stores, I baby-sat, and I took business courses and had jobs summers, so that by the time I finished high school I was ready to qualify as an experienced stenographer. I made up my mind then that if there was one thing I would have in this world it would be money. Anybody who has been as poor as we were would feel the same way."

"Would Juliana?"

"Oh, no. She was never ambitious like I was. She took things as they came. We were horrified when she ran away and married Ulysses Green. He was in his late forties and she was only a girl. He led her a wretched sort of life out on the leases in West Texas but she never seemed to mind."

"Yet the marriage broke up?"

Amanda said, "Yes. He regretted that afterwards but Juliana had got settled back here in Dallas, so she wouldn't marry him again. It was strange. He kept after her, for years. He was tenacious, I think. He had had luck in the oil fields but no luck in marriage and I guess he wanted to try it again. But Juliana never would marry him the second time."

"I asked you once before if there was a woman in the case?"

Amanda did not answer.

"Well, then, did you at any time try to keep Juliana from marrying Green again?"

"I'm afraid I did. You see, for a long time he didn't do so well, and we thought he wanted to get his hands onto the money he had settled on her."

"The three hundred thousand?"

"Yes. But after he made so much money he still wanted her and then she decided against him herself. He still had no home to take her to. He didn't want one. She would have been dragged around, just the same, living in hotels probably, and like as not he would again lose his money . . . they all do it over and over again, you know. Oh, well. Enough of that."

"One more thing. Were you to fly out to Midland this morning? With your sister?"

You would have sworn that Amanda's surprise was genuine.

"I? Why do you ask that?"

"There were two reservations on the early plane. Mrs. Juliana Willoz, and sister. Midland is near Odessa, I believe. I thought perhaps you had made the reservations, since she had no phone."

Amanda said, abruptly changing the subject, "We must talk about Iles. He has gone away. It looks very bad, to the police, or will when they know it. Did he tell you he was going?"

"No, he did not. He was to see me this morning at seven. He did not show up."

Amanda said, after a moment, "Iles fired that shot. Last night. The one from Kim's gun."

I avoided looking at her. What she had said was horrible. He wouldn't've gone back on her, I thought, remembering the elaborate attempt to keep Amanda out of the picture by recovering the flying red horse.

"Since he has not seen you I must tell you about it. I made him very cross because I bought these ruby clips. They were an extravagance, but I made the money on a deal of my own, and I thought it was none of Iles's business. Usually he makes no objection to anything I spend, anyway, because I have my own budget and he knows very well that I always make my own money pay its way, and that if I indulge in a few minks or rubies—they're my passion—now and then, I've earned them in some other way. But Iles got on a high horse about these clips. I knew why he was angry, but I pretended not to notice. He also dislikes Lucius Brady."

"That was obvious," Patrick said.

Amanda went right on. "The minute you left last night he started scolding me about the clips. He came upstairs and made a scene—it only lasted a minute and he had been drinking and he had something else on his mind. He went back downstairs almost at once. Then he stepped outside and shot off that pistol."

"What pistol?"

"Kim's. Kim left it at our house. In his overcoat pocket."

"Why didn't Iles tell that to the police?"

"Oh, he will. When he comes back."

"You don't know where he is? Yet you say he'll come back?"

"Of course he will. Iles is a perfectly honorable person."

"But if he shot the shot that killed your sister . . ."

"He shot up in the air," Amanda said.

Patrick said, "All right. Please go on."

"I was up in my bedroom. Iles stepped out of the bar and fired off that big automatic. It was right under my window. It gave me a frightful scare. I thought he had shot himself. I rushed down just as I was. I had not undressed, and I ran out by way of the terrace, and just then Iles closed the door of the bar and locked it, so I came back in and walked across the living room to ask what was wrong. He said he just shot off the gun for the hell of it. Then I discovered that I had dropped a clip. He said he would get it and went outside."

"Nobody else heard the shot?"

"Sally and Rosemary were in the other wing. Sally later took the dog out and I don't think either of them heard the gunshot, or they probably thought it a car backfiring over on the boulevard, if they heard anything at all. And, anyway, Iles shot high in the air. He couldn't possibly have killed Juliana."

"Unless the bullet ricocheted."

"In that case," Amanda said, "why would it have gone entirely through her head?"

Patrick said, giving her a long level look, "Exactly what do you think I can do to help you, Mrs. Dollahan?"

Her rigidity broke down.

"That police detective, Tisbury, is very impressed with you, Mr. Abbott. I think you can talk him into discontinuing this investigation entirely."

Her suggestion was fantastic. I looked at Patrick quickly. He did not return my glance. He was looking at Amanda, his gaze level and unchanging.

"It can either be an awful mess, a rotten scandal simply ruining our lives, or it can be an accident. I want it to have been an accident. Juliana walked in a badly lighted area very late at night. An accidental shot killed her. But it wasn't fired by Iles, from Kim's gun. It was just a shot from . . . anywhere."

"You think I can make that stick with the police?"

"I know you can, Mr. Abbott."

"Thank you," Patrick said stiffly. "And just whom are you trying to protect?"

A most startling thing happened. Tears welled up in Amanda's velvety black eyes and ran down her smooth pale cheeks.

"My husband," she said huskily. "I know I am not at all demonstrative but I do love Iles with all my heart."

13

PATRICK refused to go shopping with me, but he walked with me to Neiman's. I walked proudly, as always when he was with me, and I did not walk too fast, because partings from people you love are sad, even when for only a short time. And if I believed in hunches, and maybe I do, I also may have been worried, because I kept trying, though knowing it was no use, to get him to come with me.

"It's no good. Just about the time your fittings would get interesting the salesgirl would turn me out. Or put up a polite screen."

"We could have her leave."

"It doesn't work. The partitions seldom go to the ceilings, and the doors are always opening because somebody is looking for a fitting room."

"The excuses you dream up! Neiman's is famous for its handsome and very private fitting rooms. And their girls would always knock before they enter."

"Not the customers," Patrick said. "And the damned customer is always right."

"In other words you hate shopping."

"You hit the nail on the head."

"Don't be sarcastic, Pat."

"Then stop trying to nag me into doing something I hate doing. Shop, my love. Blow our wad. But don't ask me to tag along."

It was a heavenly morning. The air was truly like a pale colorless wine. The sky was very blue and cloudless. The sun was shining with just the right amount of warmth. The steady little wind was blowing. Everywhere you saw girls and women beautifully dressed. The men looked less so. Patrick declared that the men you saw in San Antonio dressed more to his taste. There, he said, you saw more of the ranchers, tall and lean, wearing the gray or faun-colored suits which were right for the ranch country, and wearing with great style their small pale Stetson hats. Dallas was a woman's town, but really he didn't mind that. Come to think of it he liked to look at women, so long as they didn't nag him to go shopping.

"But what will you do all morning?"

"Think."

"Well, think about Sally while you're thinking. Crazy kid, with that gun."

"I'll think about her, then."

We had arrived at the Commerce Street entrance of the famous store. Patrick consented to walk inside and took a hasty look around and sniffed politely of the perfumed air and then said, "Now, enjoy yourself. Buy everything you want and what the hell."

I am the tight one, and already my nature was starting a resistance against possible extravagance.

"If I did blow it you wouldn't turn a hair, Pat. That's a swell quality in a husband. Except it finally works out you go on relief. Bye, now."

"Bye."

I took a step and turned back. "Oh, where shall we meet?"

He was gone already. He had run like a rabbit the minute he had a chance. He always behaved thus in shops. I went on and for a while thought nothing more of it. I must try to get back to the hotel, though, before he went out to lunch with Rosemary.

No, it might be better the other way around. I smiled when I thought of Sally and me walking in on Pat and Rosemary at Mario's. The thought gave me a sadistic sort of amusement as I prowled about the store, first looking, and then settling down to buy, starting of course with the lingerie.

Shopping in this store was a pleasant experience. The salespeople behaved like hostesses. Nothing was too much trouble.

I blew myself to a couple of things made of pure silk and beautiful lace. In the sports shop I bought some swanky denims suitable for New Mexico. All purchases were to be sent to the hotel. Presently I had only a half hour left and I returned to the main floor to buy stockings and a pair of evening slippers.

It was about then that I started feeling uneasy. The shopping binge had taken my mind off the murder case for a while, but now it went back, doubly urgent. I found a public phone and called the hotel and asked for Patrick Abbott.

The telephone buzzed vainly in what must have been our unoccupied rooms.

I asked for the desk. Yes, the key was there. No, Mr. Abbott had left no message. Thank you, ma'am. Good-bye.

Checking the time I wondered why I was so foolish to be worrying, and I went to the shoe salon to choose the slippers.

The salesman took off my right pump and measured my foot for size. I told him what I thought I wanted. He went away to fetch a selection for my choice. I lit a cigarette. I wondered what Patrick was up to. I wondered also why I hadn't stayed with him, instead of taking this precious morning for my shopping. I could have shopped this afternoon, or tomorrow, instead of being so set in my ways that I imagined I had to do it just as I had planned. Come to think of it, he had been glad to be rid of me. Why?

"May I join you, Mrs. Abbott?"

The smooth melodious voice did not even make me start. It slid in like something in a daydream. It was persuasive. There is definitely something very personal about buying shoes, yet it did not occur to me to mind his joining me.

I said, "If you don't mind sitting in on shoe shopping, please do."

He assured me that he enjoyed it. Shoes were like jewels these days. It was a pleasure to buy them, he would think. Men had no choice. Fashion decreed, and man could digress but slightly. The clothes of women, however, especially the new styles, were magnificent.

Brady was wearing glasses with heavy dark brown frames and thick lenses. They took away to some extent the dreamy charm of his eyes.

He was dressed in a light gray suit, a splendid but elegant necktie, and a white shirt. He took a cigarette from his thin gold case and lit one of his special cigarettes with his gold lighter.

The odd thing was the way he made me feel. It was exactly as Patrick had said. I immediately tried to speak too precisely, for me. I was conscious of my Midwest accent. And, because Brady was with me, I felt suddenly pleased that my stockings were fashionably sheer and of the best quality and in a stylish shade. I felt glad that my ankles were shapely. My pedicure, thinly veiled by nylon, was in order. My emeralds, in my ears and on my wedding finger, were, I rejoiced, of the best quality.

I was happily married. I was a mother of a son. I was as adult as I could ever hope to be, I suppose, yet I was pleased that such superficial items could not help but win the approval of the exquisite Lucius Brady. In short, I am slightly dimwitted.

Women! I think now, remembering this. And by women I mean me. What was different in me from Rosemary? From poor Juliana? From Amanda? Even Amanda fluttered slightly when Brady was around. Brady would appreciate the full measure of her wondrous chic. She would adore that.

"Shoes are wonderful this year, Mrs. Abbott," he reiterated.

"Yes. And insanely expensive."

"But they're worth it. They can make an ordinary gown glamorous. If I may say so, you have beautiful feet. But even if you hadn't, the shoes this year could turn the trick. They make bad ankles good and lovely ankles like yours even lovelier."

If Patrick should make a speech like that, in that fashion, I would ask if he'd been drinking. When Brady did it I simpered.

I said, "I'm buying gold evening shoes. Not very original of me, I'm afraid."

"They are wonderful for evening. Classic. But vulgar as sports shoes on the street."

"A strange vogue," I said. It didn't sound like the kind of thing I say, ever. In a moment I'd be imitating one of the *ultra* sections of New York.

"Quite. It will pass, thank God. The gold evening shoe will always be good. Your emeralds are set in gold. Your rings are gold. Gold suits you, Mrs. Abbott. Your eyes, if I may say so, are almost golden. You can't go wrong if you dress to suit such beautiful eyes. "

"Thank you." Flutter, flutter!

"I noticed your emeralds last night. I wanted to say then how exceptional they are."

"Except in number," I said. Then I said, "That's my fault. I have to hold my husband back from buying emeralds. They are his weakness."

"A very fine weakness, if I may say so." Brady's wide mouth curved in his attractive smile, showing his excellent teeth. His lips had a slightly crinkly skin, which stretched smooth as silk when he smiled. "I thought about you young people after I returned to my hotel this morning. If I may say so, you seem so happy. A happy marriage is the most enviable thing in this world." He sounded actually as if he meant it, too.

"I agree, Mr. Brady."

"Yet you both have character. You're each an individual in his own right, if I judge you correctly."

"Definitely, we fight," I admitted. "But we always make up."

He smiled. "I'm afraid I'm speaking rather personally. I was impressed with you both. By the way, will you dine with me tonight?" My hesitation registered instantly. "Most informally. We'll have a private dining room. Because of poor Juliana. I've invited the Dollahans and Rosemary Willoz. It will be good for them to get out of that house tonight."

"I'll ask my husband, Mr. Brady. As far as I know we are free."

"Thank you. At my hotel, by the way. About eight." He smiled and added, "No doubt Lieutenant Tisbury will be listening at the keyhole. We'll pretend he's not there."

The salesman had arrived with a tall stack of shoe boxes. He set the boxes on the floor just as they were and started showing the shoes, beginning with the top box. He would lift the lid, take out a slipper, hold it up for my approval. I kept shaking my head and he would then put the slipper back in the box and replace the lid. The stack he had shown grew because so far he had nothing which exactly pleased me.

"I'm afraid I'm fussy," I apologized. "None you've shown me are simple enough in design."

I sounded thoroughly stuffy. Apparently I was trying to talk like Amanda.

"We got plenty more, ma'am," the salesman said. He gathered up the many boxes and disappeared to fetch others.

"Your taste is perfect, Mrs. Abbott."

Suddenly I began to get some sense back. My taste is *not* perfect. I had merely made up my mind in advance about what I thought I wanted. And because Brady was present I was being over-critical. But for him, there were at least two models in that lot that I would have tried on.

I rubbed out my cigarette. At once he offered me one of his, and I refused it. I felt annoyed because I had been pretentious and silly.

"You are very kind to let me sit with you here, Mrs. Abbott," he said then, and in a rather humble tone. "I was quite excited when I spied you here. I feel utterly wretched about that business last night. I somehow need someone to talk to about it. I can't go to Rosemary or Amanda, because naturally they are ill with grief. And I can't talk to outsiders, because they would be so morbidly curious about the affair. But you were with us last night. You were part of the evening which ended in such tragedy."

Now I was listening hard. No longer would I take even an ephemeral offense, no matter what he said.

"I blame myself entirely, Mrs. Abbott."

I looked at him, astonished. He had taken off his glasses. He was tapping them against one cheek. He looked the picture of woe.

"If I had not taken Juliana's car she would not have returned to the Dollahans' on foot, and the accident would therefore not have happened."

"Oh," I said, deflated. "I suppose it was in the cards."

"You are a fatalist?"

"When it comes to accidental death. If the victim had been a few feet this way, or that way, or this and that, it would not have happened. Murder is different, of course. Premeditated murder, I mean. In Juliana's case there seems to have been no motive. She was killed, if everybody's theory is right, simply because she happened to be in the way of a bullet. She couldn't have realized a thing. And all evening she had been so happy."

"Quite."

"If I were going to die, I'd like my last evening to be full of gaiety and good wine and good friends. That happened to Juliana, I think."

"You're quite the little philosopher, Mrs. Abbott."

Inside I squirmed. I am not little, except across and around, in the midriff. I work to keep like that. I am tall and square-shouldered. I had asked for it, though. I was talking like a fish.

My only advantage was that I was rapidly ceasing to be mesmerized by Lucius Brady.

"She was ecstatically happy all evening except for her quarrel with Amanda, Mr. Brady."

He said, "I wish she had mentioned that quarrel to me." Then she hadn't? "I know how close they are, and I would have taken her back at once so that they could make it up. Juliana usually gave in, of course. Amanda gets her way, but she's the one with brains, and the other two knew it and, in spite of kicking the traces now and then, they have always let her advise them. In this case Juliana's lawyer had asked her not to talk. But she had to tell her news to somebody. So she told me. She had ceased to care anything for her former husband so her inheritance was exciting without much grief. Now, I'll tell you a secret. I promised to fly out with Juliana today to see her lawyer. It was practicable for me, because I could combine it with a business trip in Midland. She had already booked on the daylight plane. She said that she had planned to confide in Amanda and had also reserved a seat for her. But she wanted me to go instead. I have known the girls six or seven years. I know a good deal about them. Their father was a railroad worker, of Slavic descent. He never learned English. Their mother was French. Amanda worshipped her mother. Mrs. Willoz was ambitious for her daughters. Amanda is eleven years older than Rosemary. Rosemary looks like her mother and as I said Amanda worshipped her mother. The other two look like the father, who seems to have been something of a dolt. Amanda had drive and the mother, had she lived, would have realized her ambition through Amanda."

The salesman approached and Brady wound up by saying, "Amanda is what I would call wonderfully successful. She has got herself position and money, which she wanted, and along with it she's in love with her husband. You can't do better than that."

Brady seemed to set store on happy marrying, I was thinking, as the salesman set down another stack of boxes and started displaying their contents. The first slipper in this series suited me perfectly. He eased up the sole and slipped it onto my right foot and fastened the slender ankle strap.

"These are exactly right," I said.

The man smiled as cheerfully as if I had taken the first pair he showed me.

"Let's try the other, ma'am, and then have a look in the glass."

Brady said, as I walked in the slippers, "They are beautiful."

"Thank you," the salesman said. "I've several others . . ."

"No," I said. "These are what I want. I haven't any charge account, so I'll pay for them and will you please send them to the Hotel Adolphus."

The man put my pumps back on my feet and the slippers in their box. He went for his book.

"Amanda has spoiled Rosemary, hasn't she, Mr. Brady?"

"Definitely. But essentially Rosemary is sweet. She does selfish things, but then she's sorry, and she makes it up. She has a better brain than you may think. Rosemary is all right, really."

"Were the ruby horses your idea, Mr. Brady?"

"No. Amanda's. She wanted something that would not be banal. That takes taste, for the subject itself, though piquant in Dallas, could be commonplace. Our designers, of course, did the clips. I chose the rubies. I suggested to start with that amusing jewelry like the horses need not contain the best stones. But Amanda would have nothing but the very best Burma rubies. Of course the result is worth it."

"Here is your change, ma'am," the salesman said.

We told him good-bye and stepped out of the department and went out into the street. We walked towards the Adolphus.

There ought to be much to know from this man. Essentially he had told me nothing. I wished I could take back some useful information.

"Were the black pearls Juliana's idea, Mr. Brady?"

"No. It's a very fine necklace, worth twice that sum. I would have offered it to Amanda. But she paid so much for her clips that she didn't dare invest in the pearls. Iles is the head of his house and though she has plenty to spend he asked for an accounting on the clips."

"Then the Dollahans are not limitlessly wealthy?"

"Their money comes and goes. Amanda is the practical one. Iles puts his money back in the oil business. That's a gamble if ever there was one." Suddenly he chuckled. "I used to have a friend who married a woman from Pecos, Texas. He always said 'My wife's elemental, because she comes from West Texas.' When I see Iles I think of that. Iles is definitely elemental."

Time was short now. We were walking past the restaurant The Golden Pheasant and I could see the hotel half a block or so on. There was no more time to finesse. Plain questions were all there was time for.

"How did Juliana know about the pearls?"

"I told her about them. She told me about her inheritance on the way from the club to the hotel after dinner. She asked me on the way back to the Dollahans what she could buy for investment, and I spoke about the black pearls. Then she started talking about Amanda. She said she had always envied her sister her great style. What could she herself do to be like Amanda? She hadn't natural taste, she said. Amanda never asked advice about her clothes or jewels. She knew what to buy, without asking. So I said if she had money enough to buy the pearls she might start from there and put herself in the hands of great dressmakers and cosmeticians and so on. She got terrifically excited. In her imagination she was in Paris before you could count ten. And it was about then that she suggested my flying with her to Midland. Green did his banking in Midland, and his lawyers were there. She said she had made plane reservations and that she had been planning to ask Amanda to go with her, but that she had not been able to see her alone before we all met at their club. She was going to disregard the secrecy the lawyers had asked for when it came to Amanda, but she asked me instead, and since it was practical for me to go, I said yes, of course. She was like a child. She had never done anything, I think, quite entirely by herself. She was thrilled about handling everything herself. For I, of course, would accompany her only on the flight."

We were stopped by the traffic light at Akard Street. "That was why I took her car. I was to pick her up and drive her to the airport. I have not told this to the police. But I stayed to have that coffee Amanda suggested so that I could tell it to her and to Iles. I wanted their advice. Iles advised me to say no more than I was forced to. I should appreciate your keeping it confidential, Mrs. Abbott. By the way, a man is following us. Don't look now, but he's been tagging along ever since I left the hotel this morning. He's middle-sized, and is dressed in a baggy tan suit, and a hideous orange tie." Brady laughed as the light turned to green and we crossed. "You see, I'm detecting on him, too."

Time was now very short.

"Mr. Brady, do you think Juliana was murdered?"

"Of course not."

"But why did it happen?"

"Believe me, there is no answer, except accident. Or a homicidal maniac, which is fantastic."

We walked on. The man in tan lagged behind, lingering as if to look in the windows of the drugstore on the corner.

"Do you mind being followed, Mr. Brady?"

"My dear, I think it amusing."

He went with me into the lobby, up the footworn marble steps, and to the desk to claim my key. It was not in the pigeonhole, which made me glad because Patrick would be upstairs.

Brady told me good-bye and trotted down the steps. At the door he paused to light a cigarette.

The minute he was out of sight I ran down after him. I watched him cross the street. He hurried across against the light in order to grab a passing cab. As he rolled away the man in brown crossed after him and grabbed another cab which followed Brady's. My pulse beat wildly. Brady had tried to give the detective the slip. I wondered if he would succeed.

14

BUSY assorting in mind such information as Brady had given me, I took the elevator up to our rooms. It made several stops so I had time enough to consider each item. It didn't add up to much. Brady had repeated what Amanda had told us already about the Willoz girls' start in life. It was a typical American success story, but always good because we all like to see people succeed, I hope. Brady had said that Iles was elemental. Brady had offered Amanda the black pearls first but she had turned them down. Brady had inferred that the ruby clips had cost her a good deal, perhaps more than the fifteen thousand Iles had mentioned. Brady had been the one who was flying out to Midland with Juliana this morning, not one of her sisters. Brady had taken her car last night. Brady had been the last to see her alive and he was the only one who knew about her inheritance.

Trouble is, I thought, as I stepped out of the elevator and thanked the operator for bringing me up, that Lucius Brady has no motive. All that happens to Brady from Juliana's death is that he loses the commission on a three hundred thousand-dollar sale of black pearls.

There was something else. Brady had spoken almost depreciatingly of Rosemary. His tone had implied disinterest, and had been a little condescending. So he had her number, all right. Well, why not? He'd been around and he'd never see forty-five again probably and Rosemary was more than obvious.

Thus it was that Rosemary was on my mind and I was startled when I heard her sweet singsong voice.

She was in our sitting room. The door from the corridor stood slightly open.

"Amanda is right, Pat. I just mustn't be dragged in. She's a little old-fashioned, I guess, but maybe that's fine. She is all broken up as it is about me. That is really why I live in her house. She wanted to keep her eye on me so that this time I would make a really good marriage. All I can ever do is get married, and if I don't do all right this time Amanda will be simply sunk. She's got her heart set on a nice boy from a really good family."

"The other time didn't click?"

Rosemary sighed a long sigh.

"Honey, I thought Amanda would be just delighted. He was so rich. But she was shocked. He was too old. She was all for me having the marriage annulled, and I did. Iles is old for Amanda and I guess she wanted me to have what she had missed. But I did get some money out of the deal. Plenty, really, so that now I can marry anybody I want. And she wants me to do that, so I'll be happy forever and ever. I . . . I guess I'll get over how I feel about Kim, Pat."

"Sure you will. It's only a passing crush."

"You are a darling," Rosemary said. "So sweet."

"I've noticed that myself," Patrick said.

Rosemary's laughter tinkled like sleigh bells. A man loves to think his jokes are appreciated. Hoping my husband wasn't looking smug or something, I cringed, but managed to stand quite still and eavesdrop hard. Rosemary sighed again. "When a girl's pretty people just won't believe she has brains, Pat."

"You're lucky to have everything, Rosemary."

"Thank you, honey. As I said, I'm worried. I've come for your advice, Pat. It's letters, some letters Kim wrote me. I want to burn them, but I want to burn them when you or somebody is with me, so that I have a witness."

"That's a good idea, Rosemary. And a very generous one, too."

"I was silly to keep them, dear. I loved them so."

"Were they love letters, Rosemary?"

"Yes, I guess they were. And no, too. They could have been more passionate, I think. I'm crazy for a grand passion."

"Naturally," Patrick said.

My skin crawled. Then Rosemary said, "I want to try to fix up the trouble I made by telling that detective that Kim mistook Juliana for me."

"You have the letters with you, Rosemary?"

"Oh, no. They're at the house. But they're hidden where nobody could possibly find them."

"These war affairs, Rosemary . . ."

She cut in. "It wasn't an affair, Pat. I wouldn't . . . unless I married . . ."

She sure wouldn't, I thought, getting restless and bored. With a girl like Rosemary the price was a wedding ring and, hopefully, a fat balance in the bank.

"Well, I want to make it up to Kim now. I want to fix up any trouble I made. When the time comes, I'll help him prove he didn't shoot Juliana."

I could feel Patrick's intense interest even though I could not see his face.

"How can you do that?"

Rosemary laughed a small, malicious laugh.

"I know who killed her. That's how. But nobody knows that except you, Pat. You don't think anybody could be listening?"

"Shall I close the door?"

"Oh, no!" Rosemary said.

Patrick said, "You must be very careful, Rosemary. If you know who did the murder, the murderer probably knows you know. In that case your own life would not be safe, and . . ."

"I'm not worried," Rosemary said. "Are you sure Jean isn't jealous, Pat?"

"On the contrary. She likes for me to step out. Gives her a chance herself."

He knows I'm here, the big so-and-so, I thought, but after taking a step forward I bided my time as Rosemary said, "If you were mine, honey, I wouldn't take that chance. You're so tall and good-looking and so . . . so mysterious or something . . . you're just the right age, and you're sharp and kind of mysterious, and so masculine . . ."

I walked in.

"The guy's elemental, Rosemary." I tried to look cordial. "Hello."

"Hi," Patrick said, brazenly.

"Hello," Rosemary said, and showed her pique.

She looked exquisite. She wore a champagne-colored outfit and her hat of horsehair braid in the same delicate shade was wreathed with pale pink roses. Her pale hair shone silvery gold. Her cheeks were pink, her curved mouth pinker, in its Gioconda smile.

Her garden-party effect didn't make you want to offer condolences, but I did so.

"I dressed up like this to forget about Juliana," Rosemary said. "It's too awful to think about. Anyway, I never wear black, and something like this is just as close as I can come to looking sad." She stood up. "I must be going."

"Oh, don't mind me, Rosemary. I'm going at once."

She gave me a quick look, as if testing out what Patrick had said about our being so very modern. But she took her departure, and Patrick went with her to the elevator. With a great spurt of character I resisted accompanying them, freshened up my make-up and got ready to keep my lunch date with Sally. Patrick came back as I was settling my hat. There was a pink mouth cater-cornered on his own.

"Just look at yourself, Pat!"

"I don't have to. I left it on for you to see. Serves you right, listening outside doors."

"I didn't want to break in on your little rendezvous."

"I know."

"Did you get it out of her who did the murder?"

"No. Give me time . . . honey."

"Don't honey me, Patrick Abbott." All at once I laughed. "That silly lipstick is just the shape of her smile. I could identify it anywhere."

"Wouldn't stand up in court, Jeanie."

"There's cold cream in the bathroom," I reminded him. I followed him there while he was removing the evidence. "I saw Lucius Brady. He sat down with me at Neiman's while I was buying those gold slippers. He seemed to want to talk. He was the one who was flying out to Midland this morning with Juliana. Not one of the sisters." Patrick was listening hard, and I went on. "He offered Amanda the pearls first. He gave me the idea that she had paid more than Iles told us perhaps for those ruby horses. Now, I don't know that exactly, but if they are so very rich, and she has her own share of their money, why would there be any trouble over what those gadgets cost? It enters in though, somehow. And Brady took Juliana's car last night because he was to pick her up and drive her to the airport this morning. And he said Iles was elemental, whatever that means."

"Like me?"

"Shall we say, like Rosemary? Her line goes back to the cave woman!"

"We kept the door open."

"She did, you mean."

"Hey? Don't you give me credit for ordinary common sense?"

"You were in no danger, my love. That sanctimonious little sneak wouldn't take a chance which involved her so-called honor. I'll bet you fifty bucks she's a virgin."

"I may take you up on that."

"Nuts. Oh, the police are tailing Brady." Patrick gave me a sharp look. "He thinks it's amusing."

"Tisbury told me Brady had a perfect alibi," Patrick said. "It's interesting that he told you he was the one flying to Midland with Juliana."

"Why?"

"I don't think the police know that. Tisbury was here this morning and afterwards I went to headquarters with him. I've seen their evidence, and it certainly isn't anything to write home about. They haven't got anything, really. Except for one small thing, Brady has a perfect alibi. Witnesses remember his returning to the hotel. Both times. He was even seen when he went out the time he used the stairs. They checked up on him at the B & B Cafe, and both the cashier and his waiter recall his being there at approximately the time he said."

"Sounds too good, Pat."

"Right. Also, why do they tail him if he is not under suspicion?"

"And why did he tell me he was the one who was flying to Midland with Juliana?"

"Probably because he wanted to tell it."

"He could have told the police?"

"Maybe he did. Maybe Tisbury isn't telling that. He's a very smooth guy." Patrick then said, "Brady is trying to protect someone, perhaps. Amanda. Or Rosemary."

"It would have been Amanda that Juliana would have taken with her, except for Brady. She suddenly decided to take Brady. She was gone on Brady and maybe he was leading her on. If it happened to be a lot of money she was coming into . . ."

"Anybody home?" called a bold voice, from the corridor.

Patrick shouted back.

"Everybody. Come in, Lieutenant. Be with you as soon as I get rid of some lipstick, Tisbury."

I stepped into the living room and the police detective and I exchanged good mornings. He looked like a cat who had lapped up the whipping cream. His black eyes were dancing. His white teeth flashed. His brown face showed no signs of a tough and probably sleepless night. My heart sank because he seemed triumphant. "How are you, Mrs. Abbott?"

"Fine, thank you, Lieutenant Tisbury. Will you sit down?"

"No, thanks. I'm running right on. I hope you won't let the unpleasantness last night spoil your visit to Dallas?"

"We'll try not, Lieutenant. Is the case settled yet?"

"We haven't got a case," Tisbury said, glowing with great cheer. "The medical evidence tells us what we already knew. She had been dead only a matter of minutes and she was killed by a gunshot. The docs couldn't tell by the size of the wounds exactly what calibre gun was used, and we haven't been able to find the bullet. Mr. Dollahan signed a statement that young Forsythe's gun was in his possession at the time the woman was killed. He himself fired the one shot that had been fired, and he insists that he fired up in the air. In any case we can't tie it onto that particular shot because we haven't got the bullet. We had the little blonde's story at the time, but she has retracted it. She says she was overwrought because of shock. She is going to give us those letters to prove there was nothing in what she called an affair."

"Then the case is closed?"

"Oh, I wouldn't say that exactly. We've merely gone as far as we can at the moment. Something may turn up."

"I see. So that is why one of your men is following Lucius Brady?"

Tisbury's surprise was so perfect that I knew it was artificial. He recovered pronto.

"Routine, as we say, Mrs. Abbott." Patrick came out. "Hello again, Mr. Abbott. I just dropped over to the hotel to tell Mary Smith she can go home and be Sally Dollahan again, but find she has checked out."

Patrick grinned.

"So you knew about her too?"

"Oh, sure. We've kept a sharp eye on that young lady all along. She's so handy with the artillery. We were afraid she would do something foolish." He laughed aloud. "She'd've been smarter to have picked some other hotel. We figured she would eventually follow you people here. She borrowed an old car last night and took young Forsythe to the airport. He took the Lubbock plane, got off at Fort Worth, and there Dollahan picked him up in his own plane. Plain foolishness, of course. If Dollahan had asked us, Forsythe could have gone with him right from here."

"Where have they gone, Lieutenant?"

"Some place around Big Spring. We called on the Rangers to keep an eye on Dollahan. He and Forsythe arrived around daylight and went off out on a lease. Some monkeyshines about some oil, I reckon. Nothing to do with the murder case. If an oil man has some scheme going, hell and high water can't stop him till he's good and ready. And dynamite couldn't make him talk."

Patrick said, "Have you looked into my suggestion that Mrs. Willoz was shot from the opposite bank of the creek?"

"Sure. Trouble is that the only people who could have done it were you Abbotts, Mr. Brady, and Kim Forsythe." The teeth glistened friendlily. "We figure you two wouldn't, and that Brady had no possible motive even though he could have made himself the opportunity, and Dollahan's statement about the gun, if true, lets Forsythe off. Just as you said, Brady allowed himself a little too long to drive from Mrs. Willoz's house to the hotel. But he is very nearsighted and he said he hadn't got his glasses so he got lost on the way in. Brady hadn't any possible motive. He even stood to lose a fat commission on those black pearls because the prospective buyer was killed."

We went down with the lieutenant in the elevator.

"Did you get a report on Ulysses B. Green?" Patrick asked.

"Died a natural death, if you call fish poisoning natural. They dug him up early this morning and did a post mortem. Everything was on the up and up there. Said to have left a good hundred million bucks. Goes to her sisters. Well, be seeing you folks in church." He paused. "What did you mean, asking Brady what his intentions were towards Mrs. Juliana Willoz?"

Patrick grinned. "I wanted to see if anything could bother him, Lieutenant."

He strode away, healthy and full of the joy of life for some reason.

Patrick said, "Where are you going now, Jean?"

"To lunch with Sally. Why?"

"How about meeting me here around two or two-thirty?"

I said it suited me fine and stepped into a waiting cab. Patrick hailed another immediately and as it passed us he waved. It flashed out of sight at the first stoplight. I told my driver to take it easy. I wanted Patrick and Rosemary to get to Mario's before I did.

I kept smiling happily at the look I anticipated on Patrick's face when I walked in on him and Rosemary.

15

THE CAB took me to Mario's. I paid no attention to the route. It would have done me no good even if I had. I remained always completely turned around in Dallas. As I look now at a map of that city, I can see why it is so confusing. It looks like a crazy patchwork, a tangle of sections where streets run neatly, meeting like the sections of a badly-cut pie in a narrow, irregular heart.

The cab driver knew his way about, obviously, and pulled up in a very few minutes at a restaurant on a busy street. Mario's was five, or ten minutes at the most, I should say, from the Hotel Adolphus.

It was not astonishing, really, that Lucius Brady, nearsighted Brady, especially if driving without his specs, should have got lost even in an area he might know quite well, and at night. If you consult a map of Dallas you will see that it would be surprising that he, or any out-of-towner, could get around as well as we had. The answer for outsiders in this town, I was thinking as I paid the driver and tipped him, is a Nichols Brothers cab.

Mario welcomed me to his restaurant and when I mentioned Sally Dollahan he said she had reserved a table but had telephoned that she might be a few minutes late. Mario took me to the table and brought me a glass of sherry and gave me a light for a cigarette. I would have preferred a Manhattan or a martini, but just try to get one outside of a private club in Dallas.

Our table was towards the front of the restaurant. After a minute or two I looked around, very casually, because I was planning to look surprised when I caught Patrick's stern eye. First, I saw Rosemary.

Or rather I saw her champagne-colored coat and her pale shining hair showing under the crownless champagne-colored hat with its wreath of pale roses.

Her protective coloring was clever. With her blonde prettiness she would have drawn much more attention in the black she said she never wore.

My waiter arrived, set down a glass of water, and gave me another message. Miss Dollahan had been detained. She suggested that I go right ahead and lunch. She would be here as soon as possible.

It was a dreary message, and it put me in a hell of a spot.

Without Sally to back me up, Patrick would never in this world believe that I had not deliberately followed him here . . . which, of course, I had done, only I didn't want it to look like that.

I decided to have the soup the waiter recommended, and agreed to the scallopini merely because he suggested it. I was very uncomfortable mentally, to say the least.

"Another glass of sherry, ma'am?"

"Thank you."

Now, why had I done that? Sherry makes me fuzzy. Obviously I was missing on a couple of cylinders.

I'm licked in this deal before it starts, I thought. After this Patrick can have his tête-à-têtes. They're too painful for me.

I felt lonely and disconsolate at my front table while Patrick dallied with that hussy at the back of the restaurant.

Then I got tough and I turned boldly and looked hard, meaning to give my husband's indignant gaze tit for tat.

What happened was like an electric shock. With Rosemary Willoz was not Patrick Abbott but Lucius Brady!

Brady was half-facing in my direction. He was not wearing his glasses, for which I was grateful, because there was a chance without them that he had not recognized me. So with Rosemary's back turned I might not be discovered. But I could see with perfect clarity his expression. It was that of a lovesick boy. All his defenses were down. He was openly adoring Rosemary.

Suddenly everything was perfectly clear. It had been Rosemary for him all along!

The disparaging references to Rosemary, which were not very drastic after all, were made for a purpose. They had been tossed out as a blind. Naturally, with Juliana suddenly rich and then suddenly dead, Brady didn't want to give himself away just at this time. Rosemary would probably share Juliana's sudden wealth. Also the way he felt about the dollar would no doubt increase the love light in his dreamy eyes. It was there for anybody to see now, and a good many people were arriving. The look on Brady's face might as well have been labeled.

I would have to go back to the beginning and start all over again, in my thinking. In the beginning I had said it was Brady Rosemary wanted and I had said he would be a hard one to hook. Now it looked the other way round.

But would Brady let himself go, even if infatuated, except for Rosemary's prospective share of one hundred million dollars?

"The soup, ma'am. It's one of our specialties, ma'am."

"Oh. Thank you."

I picked up my spoon. I was fuzzy all right, but it wasn't the good sherry. I wondered suddenly what Amanda would think of that deal. Would she want her adored Rosemary to marry Lucius Brady? Brady wasn't young. Of course, he probably traveled in what Amanda would consider very choice circles in New York. Rosemary would go to Paris and places and maybe get her picture in *Life* at the same party with the Duchess of Windsor and Lana Turner and people like that. Would Amanda want that for Rosemary?

Amanda was to me an enigma. Her chic shrouded her like a disguise. Always it got between me and Amanda.

Even when I saw her with tears in her velvety eyes as she spoke of loving her husband, I was thinking of her elegance.

What was the real truth? What about the clip dropped on the terrace steps? Why had she gone outside at that time? Juliana was just at that time making her way, slowly enough in her high-heeled golden slippers, from her house, crossing the boulevard, crossing the tree-shaped bridge, following the one-way street, turning into the flagged path which edged the creek from the corner of the Dollahan grounds to the terrace steps.

Amanda knew she would come. Amanda *knew* it!

Spooning the thin soup which should have demanded my entire attention because it was sublime, I then, of all things, started thinking about Lieutenant Tisbury.

He was sharp. He wouldn't give his own game away. Not that one. That was why he pretended to be surprised when I said that the police were tailing Lucius Brady.

Tisbury knew that Brady was important to this case. Brady would lead them to its solution. They hadn't enough men to tail everybody, so they tailed a key witness, Lucius Brady. Sooner or later Brady would lead them to the murderer.

Did that let Kim out? Of course not. Tisbury probably thought that either Rosemary or Amanda knew the answers. Rosemary was the key to Kim Forsythe.

It didn't take Patrick's question about what Brady's attentions to Juliana meant to suggest to a trained man like Tisbury that Brady was a man to watch. But it was not likely that Brady would commit a murder, specially if the woman was one who, by the mumbling of the marriage formula, could bring him what the government would leave of a hundred million dollars. Texas had that community-property business. Brady needn't even worry about losing his share of the dough, once he had latched onto it by marriage.

He had either given the police detective the slip or the man was lying low outside. I hadn't noticed any man in a tan suit as I came into the restaurant. Maybe he had ducked when he saw me, thinking I might be meeting Brady.

I hadn't looked around for him, though. Spare-time detective, hitting on two cylinders, that was me.

Sally did not come. It was sad to eat such dream stuff as that scallopini alone. The green salad was in the gourmet class and so was the pistachio ice cream. I finished with a large cup of black coffee. Sally had not appeared and she had sent no more messages. Now and then I took stock of Rosemary and Brady. They seemed completely absorbed in one another. Rosemary was doing all the talking. Time for me to go, however, if I didn't want her to see me, as they left the restaurant, for their waiter was serving their coffee.

I asked for my bill, paid it, tipped the waiter, thanked Mario for the beautiful food, left word for Sally Dollahan that I was returning to the hotel, and walked out on the street. I looked around for a cab. There was none in sight. Opposite a streetcar with a queue of cars behind it had stopped for the red light at the intersection. Along the curb cars angled into the parking space. Every space was occupied, including those directly in front of the restaurant.

I looked up and down for a cab. There was still none in sight.

At the corner the light changed to green. Two passenger cars rolled by, then a cab stopped and the driver honked urgently.

"Cab, lady?"

I nodded and ran out between two of the parked cars, since already cars behind the taxicab were honking because he was holding up traffic.

The cab door opened. Another passenger stepped out and felt in his pocket for, I thought, cab fare. I didn't even look at this man. I stepped into the cab. The minute I did I sensed something was wrong. The cab looked all right on the outside but inside it was old and unkempt and smelled funny.

It was starting before I realized that the passenger who had stepped out had stepped back in. He steadied himself and sat in his corner of the seat staring straight ahead. He looked vaguely familiar.

I slanted him a direct look and caught my breath.

It was the man in the baggy tan suit, the man who had been tailing Lucius Brady. Well, for goodness' sake! Why would Tisbury want to pick me up in this fashion?

For goodness' sake?

16

THE CAB rolled along in fairly heavy traffic for four or five blocks and then angled to the left. I hadn't the smallest notion where we were. Even if I had watched my environs on the way out to Mario's it would have made little difference. It was one of those sections of the city which look like others of their kind everywhere. At first we were in a factory area. There were small factories of different kinds, with now and then a dairy or a laundry. Then we left the main drag and slid into a residential section. Here were small bungalows and cottages, with narrow lawns, and shade trees, and bikes and tricycles on the sidewalks and in the drives. Now and then one would be gay with spring flowers but this was an exception. It was futile to try to orient myself. This was a working-class district, and any house on any of the streets we kept to for some time could have been picked up and set down in St. Louis or Chicago or probably even in Fort Worth and you wouldn't know it came from Dallas.

The thing that puzzled me most was the smell I had got a whiff of as I got into the cab. It grew stronger all the time. Gradually it pervaded all the air in the small enclosed space. It was nauseating. And it took me back. Where? What was it? Where had I smelled that smell and been told what it was, and why did it touch me with horror and disgust?

It was funny that I couldn't place it. Not so funny at that after I remembered what it was, because the only time I had ever smelled that smell and knew what it was had been several years ago in San Francisco. It was a smell you would not be surprised at in San Francisco, but strange in Dallas, Texas.

The cab moved on, picking its way almost daintily through more residential sections, some of them handsomer than others, but all more or less the same in their outside equipment. Venetian blinds sometimes took the place of roller shades. Cars of the cheaper varieties, if any kind of car can be called cheap nowadays, continued to stand outside the houses and here and there you'd see a stuffed panda in the front yard, or a doll carriage, or a bicycle.

Homes. The homes of home-lovers, the good, the law-abiding. Homes being paid for. Homes where the children were still young, with washings on the lines in the bright sunshine. In short, the driver was keeping to parts of the city, any city, where you were least likely to encounter the police. Patrolmen are not needed very often where people are busy and happy.

This idea hit me like a rock. With it the smell seemed to become more acute. I slid another glance at my companion. There he sat, motionless as a sack of grain, looking straight ahead. His skin was pasty. He wore an old brown hat on the back of his head. The tan suit was filthy. The man's hair was thin and brown and he had a queer spoon-shaped nose, that is, with a scooped-out bridge and thick and round at the tip. His ears were flat and thin and pointed at the top and the bottom. Even the usually incurved edge of the ear was flat. The ear towards me was dirty. The ears were outrageous because of their ridiculous size and shape and their flatness, and because they were so unclean.

Suddenly I recognized the smell.

I had smelled it in a cheap rooming house in San Francisco. Patrick had said to the old room clerk who slept on a cot behind a wicket that once in a while a certain roomer put a wet blanket over his door, didn't he? The clerk had answered that as long as roomers paid their rent he didn't pry into anything they did.

It was the smell of opium, the kind of smell it gives off when it is smoked.

It came from the man beside me. He wasn't a police detective at all. He was an opium addict. I had been snatched.

In a panic I slid forward and reached for the handle of the door. The man beside me came alive, grabbed my wrist, and shoved me back in the seat. For a moment his left hand clasped my wrist. The nails were dirty. The fingers looked puffy but strong as steel. The car rolled serenely along.

We entered a park and continued to move at the legal rate of speed. It was all very decorous.

I looked then for the name of the cab driver and the number. It was a little late to think of that. I had been ticking much too slow all the time.

There was nothing at all in the frame for that purpose on the back of the driver's seat. The car had been built for a cab but it was no longer legitimately a cab.

That settled any and all rosy illusions. I had been kidnapped. I had to figure some way out.

I could only blame myself. I had walked right into the trap. Because Brady had thought so, I had thought this lump beside me was a policeman. Why had he switched from Brady to me?

The answer to that one was perfectly obvious. Sally Dollahan. Sally hadn't turned up to keep her appointment at Mario's. She had never intended to. She had sent the man instead. The men I should say, since the driver was part of the setup. They had waited for me outside and I had walked right into the net.

Why had they done this? To take Patrick out of the picture, of course. Pat would have to stop everything now and look for me. The Dollahans would then be free to run their own show, the way they preferred to. They had already got around Tisbury. By grabbing me they'd get rid of Patrick.

The idea was appalling. I had done it again, got myself in a spot just at a time when I should have kept out of the picture. Patrick would be fit to be tied.

We were approaching the edge of the park. I saw a traffic light ahead. It was green, changing to red. That was a busy street with plenty of traffic. The driver slowed down, meaning to take it easy so that he wouldn't be caught by the next red.

I sat tense. He would have to take it very easy crossing what looked like a main street. There might be a traffic officer on duty near the light. I sat waiting, motionless, waiting to jump out of the car if we happened to hit the red light, meaning in any case to make a fuss and attract attention. The green light was like a beacon. I was tight inside with hope.

It turned red. We were only a little way inside the park. We would have to make a stop.

Suddenly another drive turned to the right. The driver made the turning. He was going to roll around this park until he could leave it on a green light. He wasn't taking any chances on stopping.

I felt blank. What now?

I must have shown my resignation in my face, for I caught the driver watching me in the rear-view mirror. I could see only one green eye. It was almond shaped and astonishingly shiny. When it caught me looking it gleamed. I looked away and after a moment examined the driver himself. He wore an old cap and a sort of raincoat. The back of his reddish hair was cut off square and his neck, freshly shaved, was seamy and rawly clean, but his old cap and the coat looked dirty.

All at once the car angled to the left and put on speed and we shot across under a light which turned yellow as we reached it. We were out of the park.

We moved on through another residential section. Larger houses. Larger cars. Larger stuffed pandas inside, no doubt, and colored maids, more money, and policemen scarcer than ever.

Inside me grew a hard knot of anger against Sally Dollahan. It was not a passing thing, like last night, when she accused me of playing a dirty trick on her father by calling the police. Now it was definite. Sally had done this and somehow or other I'd get even. I reviewed our short acquaintance. That first impression hooked me, there outside the hotel. I loved her because she had loved my dog. I had loved her looks. She was tall, she looked healthy and happy, she was with that nice boy. I remembered her in her room, the nice room of a normal ex-college girl. I had shared her distaste for people like Rosemary and, though she did not say it, also for women like Amanda. She had seemed my kind of people. I had liked her father. Even when Sally had come into our bedroom there at the hotel, and had stood in the half light tossing that darkly shining gun back and forth from one slim brown hand to the other, I had liked her.

Well, this time she had gone too far. I didn't like being snatched. Patrick wouldn't like it either. He wouldn't like, especially, her having picked a dope fiend to do the job.

Maybe she didn't know that. There I went, making excuses again. Most opium addicts in this country don't smoke it. I happened to recognize the smell because in one of Pat's cases I had accidentally gone into a wretched hotel that was a haven for such people. If Patrick hadn't been with me to explain it I wouldn't have known what the smell was. It was acid, pungent, sickening.

"Where are you taking me?" I asked.

It was the first time anyone had spoken. My voice was queer.

He made no reply. I met the driver's eye in the rear-view mirror. It gleamed.

I took what comfort I could in secret knowledge.

The Dollahans, Sally and maybe Iles, were back of this all right, but they would not let these people do me physical harm. There was a kind of consolation in that.

We rolled on. Surely nobody has ever been kidnapped with such decorum. We kept to the nicest streets everywhere. The houses now were again modest. The cars in the drives even cheaper. Our driver must be thoroughly familiar with the city. He never took us through a shopping center of any kind. When he came to a stop sign he managed it with a kind of quick curtsey and then rolled on. He managed to avoid all traffic lights except the one outside the park.

I watched for the stops, hoping that just by accident a cop would be close, but no such luck.

At last we rolled down a slight slope and the driver slowed so as not to be stopped by another traffic light on ahead. It was red changing to yellow.

Suddenly I knew where we were. There was the creek. On our right as we crossed the bridge was the waterfall.

I leaned forward to look out to see if I could glimpse the Dollahan house. The man in tan reached out a hand and pushed me back into the seat.

We caught the green light expertly and made a left turn.

There was a cold comfort in knowing where I was. As we followed the boulevard on into the park I was thinking that this ride had to come to an end some time and if it were soon I would know about where I was. If I could get word to Patrick . . .

Then my chest grew tight with excitement. On ahead was another traffic light. It was red and we would make it on the green. But perched beside it, and on our side of the street, was a motorcycle cop.

My excitement ended abruptly. The man in tan took me by the back of the neck and forced me down against the seat. My face was squashed against the worn, dirty upholstery. My arms were pinioned by one of his hands and the other covered my mouth. The car moved past the officer, as smooth and stately as if part of a funeral procession. We crossed a boulevard and then made a left turn.

The man kept my face down upon the seat until the driver changed gears and turned into a drive and stopped the car.

I was permitted to sit up. Now I was furious. I settled my hat and got out my handkerchief and then I looked out and my anger turned to stark cold fear.

We were parked behind an old paintless clapboard house. It looked vacant. There were no shades. The panes of the windows were gray from accumulated grime. The back stoop was rotting away. A wooden box served as a step to the rotting back porch.

A wistaria vine which grew up the back of the house was putting on some tiny leaves. It had the only look of life in a backyard which was only about twice as large as the car, and which existed in a permanent gloom because it was surrounded on three sides by windowless brick buildings that looked like warehouses several stories high.

The driver got out and opened the door.

"Here we are, ma'am," he said.

Now I didn't want to leave the car. It seemed a haven, compared to the deserted, tumble-down house.

"Get out, ma'am." That courteous "ma'am" was deceiving. I decided to argue it out.

"Look..."

The man beside me grasped my shoulder and pushed me towards the open door.

"Leave her be, Ed," the driver said. "Step on it, ma'am. We ain't going to hurt you. We even got a lady upstairs to see after you." Then he made a joke. "We like to keep these things clean, ma'am."

I stepped out of the car. I smelled Mexican chili, and train smoke.

"What is this place?" I asked.

The driver had a face like a rat with green eyes.

"A Mr. Dollahan pays the taxes, ma'am."

"That's just what I thought. But why pick me?"

"Come along, ma'am. There's nothing to be scared of."

The one called Ed took me by the arm and walked into the house and up a flight of bare stairs and along a hall. The driver strolled after us. At the back end of the hall he stepped ahead and opened a door into a room which was entirely bare save for a couple of chairs and a camp cot. The lady he had mentioned sat on the chair. She was Amanda Dollahan.

17

Amanda was dressed as she had been early this morning at our hotel. She wore her million-dollar black suit, the white blouse, and at her throat were her ruby clips. In her ears were large earrings shaped like flowers and set with rubies. Her hat was black with a veil which could float at the back or be tied under her chin. Her gray hair showed in front in immaculate adjustment, as if she had just come from the hairdresser. It had looked like that last night however, and also this morning. Amanda had a gift for looking as though cleaned and pressed and just turned out of the folded tissue paper.

The two chairs were the kitchen kind and the paint, originally gray, had worn off. All semblance of finish was gone from the floor. The walls had once been papered in a cheap patterned paper and the paper had yellowed and the pattern remained only here and there. Water stains ballooned under the windows. In one corner old yellowish plaster had fallen off showing bare lathes. The place smelled rotten, like all decaying houses. No doubt termites were working away right under our feet.

"Sit down," Amanda said.

She chose one of the chairs, the one nearest the door to the hall. That left me the one nearest the window. This seemed a break, at first.

Taking my time, I got out my cigarettes, offered her one, and when she shook her head, gave myself a light. I walked over to the window. Through the film of grime I could see the blue sky above the windowless buildings which all but engulfed the house. The porch below was not a porch really, having no roof. It was more like the widening of a stoop. The thick trunk of the wistaria vine was *not* within reach from the window.

"You can't get out that way," Amanda said.

I said, walking over and sitting down, "How do you know?"

"I've tried." She must be crazy, I thought. "The vine was here when I was a child."

In the sickly gray light, with her elegance, she sounded crazy. I had pictured the Willoz girls in a cottage or bungalow, like one of those we had passed on the way here in one of the respectable working-class sections. This was an eerie two-storied hovel.

Amanda said bitterly, "It was like this then. The same wallpaper. The plaster always coming off in that corner. The floor was clean, because my mother wore herself out keeping all of the house clean by scrubbing it with a pail and brush. That window was clean too because she would sit on the ledge risking her life and wash the outside painstakingly. Those buildings were there then, too. It amused me a few years ago to buy the place for a song and it amuses me now to know I can get twenty times what I paid for it. I won't sell it, of course."

"I should think you'd want to get rid of it. Forget about it."

"On the contrary. It keeps me from getting too proud."

She was a woman who talked without many gestures. She sat quietly, and straight-backed, and seldom moved her hands, which were gloved, or her feet, which were elegantly encased in pumps which had cost her what her parents probably paid in rent for this dump for a full year.

"You're putting it to a queer use now," I said.

"In what way?"

"Am I being held for ransom or something?"

"How quaint! You are merely being detained until your husband starts minding his own business. We've had as much as we intend to take."

"We?"

"Certainly we. Why not? And I must say that when we decided to make this move we were grateful to have the old house. The approach is through an area where people don't bother to be curious. They haven't the time, like you, to mind other peoples' business. And anyway they've got things to hide themselves. No one can see into this room. We could hold you here for days and no one could possibly find you."

"One of your henchmen might squeal, Mrs. Dollahan."

"No," she said.

I knocked an ash on the floor. "Sorry not to use an ashtray," I said sweetly. "What about the one that takes dope? I've always heard you couldn't trust a doper."

A strange change came over her face for a moment, then she said, "I don't know what you mean."

"The one in tan with the queer ears smokes opium."

She gave a kind of laugh. "You get around, Mrs. Abbott."

"Off and on I do, Mrs. Dollahan."

There was a tiny silence. In the next room I could hear the men talking. No, only one of them talked, and it was as if he talked to himself. There was a connecting door, which was closed, but the wood in this place was matchbox stuff, and the tone of the man's voice came clearly though the words were blurred. He must be trying to keep his voice down.

"You can trust that kind if you like," I said. "I don't. I don't know what you're up to, and I can't see what you hope to gain by it, but that rat-faced one and the one that never says anything . . ."

"He can't." She spoke as if it mattered. "He's dumb."

"You mean the addict . . ."

"You are trying to show off," she said. "You don't know what you are talking about. The men are all right. I know them both well. You will not be harmed so long as you sit here and mind your own business. If you had been brought here last night, you and your nosey husband and that nosey little mutt . . ."

I held up a hand.

"Please," I said. "Pancho has an elegant pedigree."

She ignored it. "But, no, you had to call in the police. I had to sit there in my house and see it poked and pried in and the mud and dirt brought in on the feet of policemen. I had to sit there and have my sister questioned in that fashion with you listening in because in some way or other your husband got around that lieutenant. I had to abase myself, to come to you this morning and beg your husband to intercede with that man, and to be told that he would not do it."

"You must be crazy. Patrick couldn't stop the police."

"He didn't try. Instead he went straight to headquarters and told on me. After I left you this morning. I was having you watched. I know what happened. It was then that we decided to have you picked up."

"We?"

She let it pass.

"You have been followed ever since. When you left Neiman's the man you accuse of being a dope addict followed you. You walked along Commerce Street to your hotel with Mr. Brady. You were watched. Mr. Brady took you into the hotel and came out. You came down the steps to spy on him, to see where he would go. My . . . our man saw you. He pretended to be following Brady. He merely drove around the block and went on waiting until you came out of the hotel. It was easy to pick you up where you went because it's out of the center of the city and cabs are scarce there. It worked like a charm."

"We? Do you mean you and Sally Dollahan?"

Amanda did not reply.

"Where is Sally Dollahan?"

"I haven't the foggiest idea."

"Now you sound like Lucius Brady," I said.

Amanda's black eyes snapped. "We'll leave him out of this, if you don't mind."

That made me laugh. It was no laughing matter, stuck in this awful place with this maniac and her two hirelings, but the very idea of keeping Brady out of our talk, as if it were impure, and he an angel or something, was too funny for words.

I became more cautious. I dropped my cigarette and rubbed it out with my shoe, and decided to watch my talk.

"I had a date for lunch with Sally. She didn't show up. She kept sending messages but she never came. I'll bet you collected her first. I shouldn't be surprised if . . ."

Amanda looked horrified.

"I'd sooner collect a den of rattlesnakes."

"I notice there is no love lost. But in an emergency no doubt you'd protect the name of Dollahan."

"You're really too, *too* acute."

I said, "Let's stop this, Mrs. Dollahan. Really, what can you hope to gain by keeping me here?"

"To avert a scandal. Nothing more."

"But you're making one. Right now."

"Oh, no. Already the investigation has been called off. The policeman stationed at the house has been taken away. The servants are not back, because we asked them to stay away at this time, but otherwise things seem to be normal. When Iles returns . . ."

"Do you know where he went?"

"He rang me up. He went out West about business. He'll be home tonight. When he comes everything will work out fine. The funeral will be tomorrow."

"After which, I daresay, you and Rosemary will divide up your inheritance."

"How dare you!" Amanda said, like an old-fashioned movie.

So that was a vulnerable spot. I decided to play on it. My self-confidence was growing now. I didn't suppose Patrick could possibly find me, but I felt pretty sure that Amanda wouldn't dare do anything drastic to me because she couldn't trust two men's knowing it and she was mortally afraid of scandal. And so she was touchy about the money.

"If it's a hundred million, as rumor has it, you'll split it between you, I suppose. You and Rosemary. I take it, it's not all cash, say half or even three-fourths of it is in oil properties. Texas, I hear, is pretty lenient about taxes on its oil properties. So maybe you and Rosemary will come out with, say, twenty-five millions each. Or something like that. I can't even imagine one million myself, let alone twenty-five, but I haven't had much experience in big money."

To my amazement she listened, and I went on, improvising as I went.

"Even twenty-five millions ought to look good to Lucius Brady. He lost out on the whole sum when your sister Juliana was killed, but maybe he'd settle for a part. Here in Texas you may have that community-property business, so even half of twenty-five million would set him up for life."

"You are disgusting," Amanda said.

"Why?"

"Lucius has nothing to do with this."

"Oh, yes, he has."

She sat forward in the chair. Very high and mighty again.

"I've heard all I'm going to, Mrs. Abbott. You've been snooping all along, just as I thought. It was Iles who wanted you to come to dinner. I should never have asked you myself. But there was nothing to do about it except hope that you would not accept. You began snooping the minute you came to our house. You slipped up to talk to Sally. You listened on the stairs to the quarrel. My sister Rosemary saw you. She said you came down just far enough to hear well, and then stood there and listened. You heard what I said to Juliana. You know that it was more than the pearls we quarreled about. You heard her slap me."

I said incredulously, "Heard *her* slap you?"

"Don't deny it. Because she slapped me you and that loathsome husband of yours think I shot her. You think I used Kim Forsythe's gun and shot my own sister, and that Iles is covering up for me. You think I dropped one of my clips on the steps and that he is also covering for me there. I know what you're up to and don't think I don't. But you're up against more than you can handle and don't think you aren't. If I may drop into the vernacular, Mrs. Abbott, we are running you out of town."

I was still astonished, not at her talk, or her slipping into what she called the vernacular, but because of her saying that Juliana had slapped her.

Now why would she take that tack? Because she was ashamed of having done the slapping, after Juliana was killed?

Or was she making a sort of confession? Had she killed Juliana in her high anger when she had told her Brady would marry her? Had Juliana told her then?

It was impossible to think of her killing her sister for the inheritance, because Amanda couldn't possibly have known at that time if Juliana would really inherit, or at least if it was much.

But was it for herself she wanted Brady? Or for Rosemary? Did she know he was making eyes at Rosemary?

I said, "Brady was going to marry Juliana, you know."

Her eyes veiled. She kept silent.

"Brady's getting on. That money will set him up for life. He must be tired of peddling trinkets, even glorified ruby horses and black pearls and such. He would rather have had the whole lot, but under the circumstances he would probably settle for half of what Juliana would have had. Is he in it with you, Mrs. Dollahan? It's hard to think of Brady taking Juliana, even with more dough, when he might get you . . . or Rosemary."

"You are revolting!" Amanda said, like a book.

"I don't get it," I said. "I like our Western men, men like Pat and Kim and your husband. Brady is a little, near-sighted smoothie whose chief accomplishment is to make every woman feel like a jewel in a satin box. Real satin. That's all there is to him, you know. He is as cold as a knife. Except in one way. Brady, like everybody else, has a weakness, but I didn't discover that till just lately, and I'll bet I wouldn't then if he had been able to see me across a middling-sized room. He is vain. He hates to wear his glasses when talking to a woman he's making a pass at. The specs reduce his blue eyes, make them look hard like a snake's. Without them they look dreamy and romantic."

"What rubbish!" Amanda said.

"Do you know where he is? Right now?"

"Are you accusing me of spying?"

"You spied on me."

"You spied first," she said. "I don't know where he is and I would not lower myself to ask. I daresay he's attending to his business."

"I say. He's so business-like that he's making his pitch for those millions before Juliana is in her grave. If you want Brady, Mrs. Dollahan, you'd better get a move on, because Rosemary is beating your time."

"My sister is lunching with your husband. For the express purpose of keeping him out of our affairs."

"You underestimate my husband, Mrs. Dollahan. He's stood your sister up."

This was mere wishful thinking. It made me feel good to say it, but I should have stopped there.

"Your smelly friend should have gone into the restaurant, Mrs. Dollahan. That is, if Mario would have let him come in, which I doubt. Then he could have seen and reported just where Lucius Brady is now making calf's eyes at your sister Rosemary. A stitch in time, making hay while the sun shines, that kind of stuff."

I was exaggerating. By this time they would probably have gone.

Amanda tried not to appear moved.

"How ridiculous!"

She stood up. She walked to the window. Here, I thought, possibly in this room, she learned to walk like that. With a book on her head, if she owned a book.

She gazed for a moment through the window and then without speaking to me again she left the room. She turned a key and locked me in.

She went into the adjoining room. She spoke in whispers. The one that could talk answered in mono-syllables and after a little of this she left the room and I heard her high heels tapping down the naked, paintless stairs.

I went to the window and saw her step out on the porch and down upon the goods box which served as a step and then with great delicacy she went off around the house. I was looking after her and again calculating my chances of escape and beginning to realize that I had made a mistake to talk as I had, when I smelled the smell. I whirled about. The connecting door stood open. The man in tan was watching me from the middle of the room. His eyes were small and sky blue.

18

THERE was nothing baleful in those blue eyes. There was nothing benign, either. They watched me like a bug on a pin. There was a peculiar horror in their detachment. What he had to do he would do. That was all there was to it. If Amanda Dollahan said take her by the neck, crack it like a bird's wing, it would be done. If she said open the door and let her walk out, it would be the same. She had probably told him to leave me alone at present. He did not even bother to come near me. He remained in the doorway and, having finished looking, he turned and went into the other room and closed the door again.

He closed it gently. His hearing must be sensitive. It certainly was tops. Perhaps a shrill noise would rattle him. I weighed the possibilities and decided not to experiment.

I heard the rat-faced man speak and I wondered how the dumb man answered. Perhaps they were so used to each other that Ratface understood without either words or signals. They might work together constantly and then be able to plan their deviltry with glances and gestures.

I was not as calm as this may sound. Inside I was frantic. But at the moment I was more frightened of having those evil-smelling hands laid upon me than of anything else. I sat very still on the chair and tried to think the thing out. It seemed impossible to escape. The window was hopeless. If I could have opened it or pushed it out they would have heard me and grabbed me before I could jump. If I did jump I'd break my neck. The door into the hall was locked. Even if I could get into the hall I had to pass by the door to their room to get to the stairs. The dumb man could hear the grass grow. I hadn't a chance unless Patrick found out where I was and got me out.

To pass the time I went back, all the way to the telegram Patrick had sent from Houston asking if I wouldn't drive down and meet him in Dallas. All that had happened followed on my mistake in bringing the dog. *Mistake number one.* The car door was standing open. I'd said good-bye to Mike and his nurse. Pancho had hopped in and sat up on his haunches and wiggled his little front feet. That dog had too much charm. Then the nurse spoke up. You ought to take him, she said. You know how well he guards the car. You're driving alone. Sometimes you'll strike a stretch without a town for maybe fifty miles. Maybe you'll need the dog. He's little, but that doesn't stop him. He's got a blanket in the car.

While she talked Pancho wiggled his forefeet and gazed at me so successfully that first thing I knew the door was closed and he was on his way to Dallas, Texas.

The chain of circumstance! A dog gets in a car, rides six hundred miles, gets out of the car just as a girl comes along. She is reminded of her own dog, recently murdered. As a result here I sit in an evil-smelling house chaperoned by a couple of thugs. One of them dumb, and a doper.

So far, no dice. No matter what the sequence of events, I had wound up here, without an exit.

What was Patrick doing? Would he be alarmed when I hadn't shown up at two-thirty? Would he wait at the hotel or would he try to find me? Would he turn into Superman and ferret me out in this improbable place?

Whoops, he might not have shown up at the hotel himself. Why dream?

What had happened to Sally? Had she also been picked up by Amanda's boy friends? Were the messages phoned supposedly by Sally to Mario's phoney?

There I went, making excuses for Sally. Chances were she was in with Amanda and Iles and maybe even with Rosemary. We were the outsiders, the ones who were not minding our own business when in Texas.

There was complete silence in the adjoining room. To test them out I stood up and took two steps. The door opened. I sat down again. The dumb man looked, and closed the door.

What was there to do?

Nothing.

To pass the time I took up my itinerary again, from the time I stepped onto the sidewalk and saw Sally and Kim. I walked up the steps and met Patrick in the lobby. I remembered how I felt about Iles and Amanda Dollahan. The impact of his friendly good looks and her chic.

Sally joined them, with Kim. They looked so happy. We accepted an invitation to dinner. *Mistake number two.* Amanda had not wanted us to accept. But Iles wanted us and Patrick wanted to go. It was business. It was a few hours out of my life, and any way I had no real choice. Patrick hadn't meant it when he had said damn the party, after we were in our rooms. His mind was made up in advance. Had Iles told him something that he didn't tell me? I thought not. Iles would be close-mouthed about his family. Patrick thought the problem was a family affair. He had wanted Patrick to meet the family before he talked over whatever was on his mind.

We had dined at the Club. Nothing that happened there seemed, in review, unduly suspicious, except that Sally had not come.

We went on to Brady's party in the Mural Room. It was flawless.

But how much did Rosemary and Amanda know at that time about what was happening to Juliana? She had carried her telegram in her gold kid evening bag. The bag was all over the place. Left on the table. On her chair. Once gathered up from the floor.

Nothing as far as I could determine had happened during that party that could be called anticipatory of the murder.

Rosemary had been extra long in the powder room once, but her lipstick and eyelashes called for constant renewal to remain perfect.

Kim Forsythe had abandoned the party for about twenty minutes. I had imagined this was to telephone to Sally.

Brady had been called out by a long-distance call which kept him away perhaps five minutes, and for which he was apologetic.

Amanda had been restless but not to a suspicious extent.

Rosemary had snapped at Juliana once when the older sister lifted a lock of her irresistible hair. But Juliana had a way of putting people on edge.

No, there was nothing which was a key to what happened later. The trouble had begun at the house. *Mistake number three.* We should not have gone there.

Again Amanda had not wanted us. Was it because she meant to have it out with Juliana? The quarrel was inevitable. All paths led to Amanda.

Mistake number four was stopping on that bridge and hearing the dog and going back. *Number five* for me was walking into this trap.

But such thinking was super-futile. It kept me from thinking of my plight. And it got me nowhere. What I had to do to get out of this place. If I could push out that window, take a chair to it as they do in pictures, take a chance jumping for the wistaria vine, which would at least break my fall . . . Oh, fish! What nonsense!

I had no watch. I didn't know the time. It seemed later than it was because of the deep shadows cast by those tall buildings. The dirty window looked almost opaque. Because of the shadowed light I saw a slit at the top of one pane where the putty had shrunk away. That pane could be worked loose. Maybe with luck it could be removed without attracting the dumb man. Well, a lot of good that would do me. There wasn't room for a small-sized dog to squeeze out of a space that size. It was just about right for Pancho.

I walked to the window and looked out. Below the gloom was thickening. The backs of the warehouses were deep purple. The cinders which carpeted the tiny yard were a lusterless black.

The car stood where we had left it. The vine was too far out of reach even to dream about.

I hadn't a chance. That chink above the window pane was nothing. My best bet was to sit and wait.

Suddenly I caught a certain whiff and whirled about just as fingers wrapped themselves around my arm. I gasped with horror.

The dumb man marched me back to my chair and set me down there firmly. He stood and looked. He went out.

He could hear anything. There was no escape. I couldn't even stand by a window. Perhaps he was afraid somebody would come into the pit of a yard and spy me. So long as I sat in this chair evidently he would not molest me. I settled down to sit and wait.

I waited. There was more silence. Ratface must be taking a nap. I looked at the camp cot near the door from the hall. I must not consider it. I must not go to sleep whatever else. It could happen, even here, after my staying awake all last night. To pass the time I opened my bag and began to assort its contents. Having been straightened up for the trip to Dallas, it was remarkably tidy. There were my vanity things, my purse, and a few cards given me by clerks at Neiman's. There was an advertising leaflet I had picked up somewhere. I opened it and read.

It was called *The Story of Pegasus.*

Greek mythology tells us that when Perseus, ancient Greek hero, cut off the head of Medusa, the evil spirit with brazen claws and serpents in her hair, the blood sinking into the ground produced a marvelous horse with wings. Minerva, Goddess of Wisdom, caught and tamed him. She named the horse Pegasus and presented him to the Muses, the Goddesses of Music and Song. Pegasus was as wild and swift and as buoyant in his flight through the air as any eagle that ever soared into the clouds. The fountain of Hippocrene, on the Muses' mountain of Helicon from which the Greek poets drew inspiration, was first started by a kick from this powerful stallion's hoof. Since that time Pegasus has been not only a symbol of power and speed, but also a symbol of the flight of poetic imagination.

The brave Bellerophon, another Greek hero, rode Pegasus on his eventful expedition against the fearful fire-breathing monster, Chimera, which was ravaging all Lycia. It was with the aid of the lightning flight of Pegasus that Chimera was overcome and that Bellerophon was able to accomplish many famous exploits. To the amazing Pegasus a thousand miles was an easy journey to cover in a day's time. . . .

I sighed. What I really needed was a flying red horse.

The leaflet was the only piece of paper of any size in my bag. It was printed on both sides. Folded it would slip through that crack above one windowpane. I opened my lipstick and wrote upon both printed pages. "Help! Call Police. Call Patrick Abbott at Adolphus!"

I folded the leaflet and put it where it was easy to slip out of my bag.

I slipped my feet out of my pumps. Watching the door in an agony of suspense I tiptoed to the window.

I looked again. The door was still closed.

I tried to slip the leaflet through the crack.

It would not go. A trick of light had made the space seem greater than it was. A leaflet, twice folded, was too thick to go through the crack.

I unfolded it. Its rustle was light as a wing, but I felt panicky. I knew it wouldn't go.

A card was too small. Nobody would pick it up. Nobody would pay a card any notice.

Again I watched the closed door. So far I was lucky. I made a last try with the wide open leaflet. It slipped easily through the crack just in time for a gust of wind that I didn't know was blowing to pick it up and whirl it out of my view.

Instantly I knew I had done the wrong thing. If anybody found that leaflet it would be Amanda. And then what? Torture, maybe. For who else could trace me here?

As I turned to return to the chair the dumb man opened the door. He gave my stockings a detached look and sidled towards me. He gave my face a stinging slap. He set me down hard on the chair. He pointed at the pumps. I put them on and began to weep with fury and despair. After studying for a couple of minutes he left the room again and this time he left the door open.

19

I DIDN'T venture from the chair for some time. I sat. My legs grew numb now and then. I wriggled around for exercise. Once I felt what seemed like a bug and I jerked down to dispose of it and found it was a run moving up my stocking. It was only one of several started by roughnesses in the floor when I had crossed to the window in my stocking feet.

My face kept burning from the slap. The flesh itself felt insulted and angry. The queer opium smell seemed to have been plastered on my cheek with the slap. It was so persistent now that I didn't know if it was real or imaginary.

The door into the next room remained partly open. After a while the rat-faced man started to talk again. I heard cards fluttering and the monosyllabic comments which go with a game, and sniffs, snorts, croaks, and some one-sided laughter.

"You're good, Ed," Ratface would say. "You're a good guy, Ed. Too bad you can't talk."

"Like Pancho," I thought. If only Pancho could have talked!

No flying horse came to my rescue. The dusk, which settled too early, was deepening. No footstep sounded on the cinders. No children ran to play hide and seek in the desolate courtyard behind this wretched house. The only reiterated outside noise was the sound of trains, a rush of passing wheels somewhere beyond the tall buildings and the snubby mutter of Diesel whistling. It seemed to come from the sky.

I closed my eyes. I opened them quickly. I was getting drowsy.

It seemed an odd thing that I could be sleepy and scared at the same time. But I was sleepy, and for a while I had to fight it. To wake myself

I imagined falling off the chair, or falling into a deep sleep and being given knock-out drops and then being carted away in that car which had once been a taxi.

Now and then the dumb man would look in on me. It was lucky for me that his special vice was opium. For such as him I was only a bug on a pin. And Ratface took orders from Ed.

Amanda had probably ordered them not to hurt me. Anything to avoid publicity. If I were not harmed perhaps nobody would believe my story.

The shadows in the room were turning black when suddenly I heard a soft click in the direction of the hall door. I wheeled about expecting to meet the sky-blue gaze of Ed, using for some reason the other entrance to the room.

He was not there. The door was closed. Everything was just as it had been in that direction.

I experienced renewed despair and defeat. But there must have been something. The dumb man was suspicious. He came to the intervening door with his cards in one hand. He looked the room over and went back to the game.

Twisting again to watch the other door I saw the knob turning. This time it turned silently.

It stopped. Wild with hope I cried, "Pat! I'm here!"

That was a mistake. All that happened was the sound of a table overturning in the next room and Ratface cursing.

I had jumped up. I sat down again, expecting the dumb man to walk in and probably beat me to a jelly this time.

He did not come. The silence now in the next room was ominous. It was Amanda coming back, no doubt. It was Amanda who had turned the doorknob and, finding it locked, went into the other room.

Everything was too queer. I stood up and, impossibly curious, I walked over to that other door and looked into the next room. It was as bare as mine. There were two old chairs, a camp cot, and the overturned card table, with the cards in a splash on the bare floor. It had two windows, grim and dirty and uncurtained, which looked out on another dark building of some kind. I didn't get to investigate further because the dumb man came from the hall.

I skipped back into what you might call my room, but not soon enough. He came after me. He came into the room and took me by the shoulders and shook me like a rag. My hat went somewhere and my bag flew away and burst open, spilling its contents all over the floor. He popped me down hard on the chair and then had a look out the window. What he saw in the growing dimness did not alarm him. He went back into the front room and Ratface arrived from somewhere. I heard them righting the table and Ratface cussing a streak because of the upset cards.

For the very first time then I lost all hope. It had been so bright for that instant. A miracle had happened, I had thought. My message on the leaflet about the red horse had been found and somebody had telephoned Patrick. But whatever it had been, and it was all very hush-hush, the men in the other room were not perturbed.

The card game went on. I sat listening.

Perhaps three or four minutes passed. Suddenly there was a terrific report. I saw the door-knob fall on the floor. The door from the hall then swung open and there was a smell of cordite. Sally Dollahan walked in.

Her green eyes were shining. She was carrying her pistol.

"First time I ever did that," she said. "Shot my way in, I mean."

"You did it, all right," I said. "Where's Pat?"

She jerked her head towards the other room. Sounds were numerous in that direction. I thought of our dumb friend and Ratface. I ran to have a look.

Patrick had toppled Ratface over and was taking on the dumb man. He hit the man with his fist. The man staggered but regained his stance and when Patrick whirled around to take another swat at Ratface, Ed kicked Patrick in the back. Ratface went down. Patrick turned and hit the dumb man again but had to whirl around to look after Ratface. He sent Ratface flying across the room and twisted again in time to sidestep a kick in his side. The dumb man liked to do his fighting mostly with his feet. But Patrick caught him off guard that time and a blow under his chin sent him backstepping towards the opposite wall like a dancer. It was a pretty sight. But I had to pull my eyes away to watch Ratface. Patrick was following up on the dumb man. His back was towards Ratface who was creeping on him again with an open knife. It had a blade six or eight inches long.

I grabbed a chair, knowing as I did it that I would be too late. Ratface held the knife poised.

Suddenly, and for an instant mysteriously, the knife fell to the floor. Ratface screamed and grabbed his right wrist with his left hand. Blood went flying. Not until then did my ears hum from the report of Sally's gun.

"We ought to let the skunk bleed to death," Sally said. She spoke to Ratface. "Get up and get over in that corner."

Ratface moaned and whined as he edged around the wall. The other two were fighting it out. The chairs went over. The card table went. The cards flew like snowflakes. The dope addict must be pretty strong. Patrick is pretty good in a fight and this was a tough one.

"They move too fast!" Sally said. "I'm afraid to aim for an arm or a leg for fear I'll hit Pat."

"I'm bleeding to death!" whined Ratface.

"Good riddance," Sally said. "Get that one away a piece, Pat, so I can wing him!"

Ratface made a break for the other room. Sally ordered him back into his corner.

At that moment a well-aimed piece of footwork on the part of our dumb friend laid Patrick out on his stomach. Swiftly the dumb man was on him, his hands like claws, his knees bending as he crouched to jump. To jump up and down on Patrick's back.

Sally was busy with Ratface. I threw myself frantically on the dumb man. He turned from Pat and grasped my shoulder and sent me spinning. But the diversion gave Patrick a chance to turn over. He got on his feet, and, using his head, rammed the dumb man as he came at him again in the stomach. I grabbed a chair and brought it down hard. One of them collapsed on the floor and I was relieved to see it wasn't Patrick.

"Nice going, Jean. Lucky you got the right man."

"Don't carp, dear. Do something."

"It's done."

"You mean he's dead?"

Patrick wiped his sweaty forehead with the back of one hand.

"Far from it. But he's out for a while. Keep that one covered, Sally."

Ratface was squealing about having been forced into something when he didn't know what it was all about. Patrick examined the dumb one. His hands went to his own necktie. Neither of our opponents were encumbered with such things.

"Don't waste that Sulka tie, Pat. I've got some ruined nylons. They'll do just as well."

"Better," Patrick said.

I stripped off my stockings and Patrick knotted one each about the dumb man's hands and feet. He still had not moved. Patrick then picked up the knife and helped himself to the window cord from the one window which had any. He tied up Ratface. He saved enough to reinforce the stockings hobbling the dumb man. He went through their pockets. Ratface had two more knives but neither carried a gun. Patrick collected the knives. He examined the wound last.

"Good shot, Sally. We won't use a tourniquet."

"I'll bleed to death!" the man screamed.

Patrick ignored him. He wasn't bleeding seriously, but why bother to say so?

"Have you a couple of bullets left for those tires, Sally?"

"Naturally," Sally said.

"Get your things, Jean. We've got to step on it."

"Are we going to leave them here, Pat?"

"They'll have good company soon."

I went back to the other room to collect my hat and bag. I gathered up what odds and ends were handy and joined the others at the top of the stairs. We ran downstairs and into the dark little courtyard. Sally took care of the tires. The gunshots echoed in the well shaped by the dark tall warehouses. I walked lightly with the others along the cindered drive, and with such freedom that I thought it was because of the miracle which had rescued me, but in the late afternoon light which grew brighter as we got to the street I saw that part of my freedom was due to my skirt. It had split from the hem almost to the waist. I was stockingless. What had happened to my face and hair was beyond conjecture. I wondered if I had lost my lipstick. In stylish Dallas I was a strange sight.

20

BEYOND the cindered alley which gave access to that decrepit house the whole world looked bright and beautiful. Yet it was only a commonplace street crowded with factories, stores of the less romantic variety, and now and then an old frame house in need of paint. The afternoon light still functioned out here, though, and I was free and with Patrick, and when we are together everything is perfect even at a time when we're having a fight. So I felt very happy. Even in a too-split skirt.

Pat snapped into a store to phone the police and Sally and I got into our car, which they had parked at the curb.

"Why didn't you show for lunch, Sally?"

"I got there just as you were getting into that cab."

"Cab! That's what I thought! I'm dim-witted. Why, even after that man stepped back in I kind of thought at first maybe you still had that share-a-ride business in Dallas. Like during the war. For a while I couldn't even figure out why he smelled the way he did."

"What do you mean, Jean?"

"Opium. When they smoke it, Chinese fashion, the smell hangs around their clothes and stuff. He's an addict, I bet."

"Oh, poor Amanda!"

I gave her a withering look. "She's not poor Amanda to me. Not with boyfriends like that."

"You don't understand."

"So I'm not broad-minded enough?" I said, still doing some withering. "I'm just a plain Midwest gal who happened to marry into San Francisco. We think we're broad-minded out there, too, but not enough to sit by and say *poor Amanda* when she has a gal snatched by a couple of thugs, and taken to that awful place, and slapped . . . I beg your pardon, I shouldn't've mentioned it. I'm just too narrow-minded for Texas."

"You don't know what I mean."

"I don't want to. You say you finally turned up at Mario's?"

"Just as you stepped into the cab. I happened to notice the license plate and remembered the number. I didn't realize it wasn't really a cab number until Pat said so. He started looking for you right away. That's how he found out that the car belonged to Amanda."

"Lovely. Just lovely. She even keeps the guys on wheels, then?"

"I didn't used to like her either," Sally said.

"You don't say!"

"She's my father's wife, Jean."

I said, "Loyalty is a wonderful thing, just wonderful." I piped down then, trusting that she had noticed the irony, which was about as subtle as an axe.

Well, after all, she had helped get me out. Shooting rattlesnakes is fine training for a girl who later in life is going in for incapacitating knife-tossers and I hereby recommend it.

Of course she was young. All Sally really needed was a few years being married, like me, an uncertain income, like ours, a wonderful husband, a baby and hopes for more. Then she would be tolerant, like I am.

Or am I? I was glad I hadn't said the above to Sally, just in case she did not agree.

"Any word from Kim, Sally?"

She looked worried.

"No. That was why I was late. He was to phone me when to expect him back in Dallas. We made a plan. He didn't call. I stayed at the house as long as possible and then Amanda phoned from somewhere that they had just left Abilene and I decided I would still have time to catch you at least for coffee. Mario's is over on Forest Avenue. I got there and got parked on the cross street headed towards the restaurant just in time to see you depart."

"I wonder how Amanda knew I was lunching there?"

"I told her," Sally said. "I didn't know there was anything secret about it, Jean."

"And she told Rosemary, so Rosemary broke her date with Pat and went there instead with Lucius Brady. . . ."

Sally said, "I don't know how it was worked out but I'll bet Rosemary didn't tell Amanda she was lunching with Brady."

"I guess not. There's rivalry there."

"It's not what you think, Jean."

"Glad to know that," I said icily. "Why did Iles and Kim fly away to the oil fields at a time like this, for goodness' sake?"

"That I can't tell you," Sally said.

"Sorry!" I said. I was cross all over again. "Okay. But don't you ever ask to borrow our dog again, Sally Dollahan! Getting us into all this trouble! Me looking like this! Pancho almost killed . . ."

"Please!" Sally said.

There were tears in her eyes, running down her flat honey-tan cheeks, real tears.

"It's something in the oil business. Oil men simply can't broadcast what they're up to, Jean. And they can't postpone things. That's how things are in the oil business."

I felt like saying the hell with the oil business. It wasn't strong enough, so I compromised by saying, "Fish!"

Patrick slid in behind the wheel and the key clicked in the lock. He started the motor. We moved on and turned left. The street we turned into was Cedar Springs Avenue. I gave him a quick résumé of my afternoon.

Pretty soon we passed a corner I remembered.

"This isn't the way to the Adolphus, Pat."

"We're dropping Sally home first."

"Oh. Okay, so long as we don't get back into that Dollahan rat race, Pat. I've had enough. That afternoon in that house with nobody looking for me . . ."

"If it weren't for Sally you'd still be there," Patrick said.

"Nuts! I tossed out a leaflet. The wind picked it up and somebody telephoned you. . . ."

"I'm afraid not, dear. If Sally hadn't remembered the license number . . ."

"Let her have it her way!" Sally said, airily. "Aren't those shops on the right sweet? Just this side of the viaduct, I mean. I thought of running a shop but I guess it would be too confining for me. . . ."

"You could always shoot the customer if one happened *not* to be right, Sally darling!"

"Stop it, kids," Patrick said. "We've got to stick together. I've got a hunch we're heading into trouble and pronto. Tisbury declares he's satisfied with the prowler theory. He's nothing of the kind. He merely isn't showing his cards. He's sure Kim Forsythe did the murder and he's lying in wait."

"He'll never recognize Kim," Sally said. "I told Kim to dye his hair black and buy a moustache."

Patrick chuckled.

"Whiskers would have covered him better, Sally."

"I said so too. Kim balked at whiskers. I told them there was a place in Midland where he could get a trick moustache, some barber out there would do the dye job. I want us simply to leave. Go to a foreign country, Colombia or somewhere where there is oil . . ."

Patrick shouted with laughter.

"If you want Kim's fingerprints changed Pat could probably give you an address," I said.

"Stop it," Patrick said again. "Kim doesn't need a disguise, Sally. He didn't murder Juliana. All we have to do is produce the one that did. Sally's been splendid, Jean. You know where I ran into her this afternoon? At the vet's. She'd gone there to see if Pancho was comfortable. He wasn't happy, of course. What shut-up dog is? He still can't talk, so I registered him for another day and Sally and I started tracking you down. We found you. That's done. So let's think about what's ahead. I'm worried about Rosemary!"

"For gosh sakes!" Sally said.

"Ditto!" I said.

Sally and I looked at each other and laughed out loud. We hugged each other.

"If you weren't so pig-headed, Sally!" I said.

"Ditto," Sally said.

"He worries about Rosemary," I said, with ice.

"They all do," Sally said, seriously. "That is Rosemary's special talent, getting people to worry about her."

"Hey?" Patrick reminded us.

We drove under the viaduct and were again on Turtle Creek Boulevard. It looked very beautiful. The woodsy spring smell came from the earth and trees and the flooded creek. It had gone down a little. Sally said that usually it was only a trickle and that the dam which we had called the waterfall had been built to make a beauty spot along the boulevard. We ought to stay on ten days or so and see the redbud bloom. Then Turtle Creek was a dream, she said. I loved it just as it was now, with the daffodils blowing and the forsythia like shooting stars and the trees looking so alive although their tiny new leaves were hardly more than spots of green light.

"Now, listen, kids," Patrick said. "Tisbury is lying low to give himself time. He's had the Rangers keeping an eye on Kim and Iles. I'll tell you why I'm worried about Rosemary. She's playing a double game. Take those letters of Kim's. . . ."

"Don't worry about those," Sally said.

"Why not?"

"I cased her room and found them. They are no more."

"Did you burn them?"

"I burned them and put the ashes down the drain."

"Does anybody know that?"

"Certainly not," Sally said. "I was alone in the house. It was when I was waiting for Kim to telephone. While Jean was waiting for me at the restaurant. Do you think I'd let a silly thing like Rosemary air those letters in public? They weren't anything anyway. Not anything at all."

"Did you read them?"

"Certainly. Wouldn't you?"

"Well, I'd be inclined to," I said.

Patrick grinned. "Sure she would, Sally. Go on."

He had stopped for a traffic light. The dam which we called a waterfall was a little way ahead. The water was still heavy enough to make a pleasant hum.

"Kim has written me much lovier letters than those," Sally said. "Even so, I can't say I love him because he writes lovely love letters. He hasn't much talent that way."

I said, "Brady could probably write a snappy love letter. But he'd be scared to send it, of course."

"Well, I'm glad I read Kim's to Rosemary. They didn't mean anything at all. They're just the letters a lonely soldier writes to a girl who smells like Chanel No. 5. I'm glad I read them. She can't terrorize him any more, or me either, because they told you plainly that Kim didn't love her at all." We were moving on. "She had a wall safe in her room. It was behind a picture, the way they all are apparently. It wasn't even locked. There wasn't anything there worth locking up and that's a fact. You won't tell the police about the letters, I hope?"

"Of course not," we both said. Patrick said, "You didn't leave any fingerprints, I hope?"

Sally's right hand flew to her chest.

"I forgot that! The phone rang and I about jumped out of my skin thinking it was Kim calling at last. It was Amanda saying she had got word from Iles and that they were at Abilene. To be friendly I told her I had been waiting to hear from Kim so I would now go and join Jean at Mario's. I was just then burning the letters in the fireplace in my own room. I collected the ashes, every one, and flushed them away, and . . . I forgot about fingerprints."

"Did you handle the wall safe with your bare hands?"

"Of course. What other way is there?"

"Well, don't worry about it," Patrick said.

We turned off the boulevard and doubled back across the bridge and on into the curving narrow street.

"You honestly didn't get my message?" I asked Patrick. He shook his head. "I had picked up a leaflet somewhere about the red horse. It was in my bag. I wrote a message to you on it with lipstick and pushed it out the window. The wind picked it up and carried it away. When you arrived I was sure you'd got the message."

"Sorry, chum," Patrick said. "We arrived simply because Sally remembered the license number. We found out that Amanda owned that car and I went to the house and made Amanda tell me where to find you."

"How did you manage it?"

"Very simply, dear. I told her I'd have the law on her, and when that didn't work I threatened to tell Iles. That did it pronto."

21

WE PARKED on the street and walked up the walk with its borders of daffodils and hyacinths. There was something strange in the silence which enveloped the house. Possibly this was because there had been such a lot of people around the last time I had been here.

Or maybe everything was suspicious after my sojourn in Amanda's birthplace. One garage door stood open. Amanda's car was out, Sally said. Her own—a Ford convertible—a station wagon and the town car they had driven last night were in the garage.

We entered by the front door, which Sally unlocked with her key.

"Just a minute," Patrick said.

We stood listening. There was a little purring sound which came from the basement furnace.

Sally called, "Yoo-hoo?" She got no answer.

The place seemed deserted.

"I'm surprised Amanda went away," Sally said. "She always insists that somebody be in the house, and with the help away. . . . oh, this is hardly an ordinary occasion. Something about Juliana, I guess."

We walked along the hall, looked into the living room, and looked in on the bar. There was no one about.

The house was in perfect order. Amanda had done it, or had it done, her passion for tidiness not deserting her even at a time like this. The air was fresh, thanks to mechanical devices controlled by the furnace. There were bowls of fresh flowers in the expected places.

The house was habitable, if you don't mind them too neat. But there was something wrong. Maybe it was my nerves. Maybe, I thought, catching an image of my battered self in a mirror, it was just me.

"We'd better go up and see about those fingerprints," Patrick said.

Somebody knocked on the door hard and then rang the bell, keeping a finger hard on the electric button.

"Answer it, Sally," Patrick said, and he sprinted upstairs. I knew he was heading for Rosemary's room to remove Sally's fingerprints from around the safe. I started in a vague sort of way looking for a pin to pin up my skirt, knowing that I wouldn't find one except in a proper pin place. Then Sally asked Tisbury in and the police lieutenant's deep baritone said thank you.

As he walked in I called upstairs, "Look in Sally's room for a pin for me, will you, Pat. A couple of little safety pins will do."

"Hello, Mrs. Abbott," Tisbury said cordially. He looked me over. "You been in a wreck?"

"I took a tumble," I said. "I'll have to borrow something from Sally to go back to the hotel in, if I can't pin myself up properly. Pat's up looking for pins."

"You have an accommodating husband, Mrs. Abbott."

"He's perfect."

"I think I'll go up and help him," Tisbury said.

I said, to gain time. "I think he can find his own pins, Lieutenant."

"Even in a haystack, probably," Tisbury said. And he sprinted up the stairs.

"Curiosity and the cat," I said to Sally. "Just because Pat's upstairs Tisbury has to go too!"

Sally said nothing. Her small tanned green-eyed face was a sphinx.

Above there was a prolonged silence. Patrick was silent when he was joined by Lieutenant Tisbury. Now both were silent. There had been no greetings. Only silence.

So I hurried upstairs. Sally came along too.

The two men were in Rosemary's room. Rosemary, in a sky-blue quilted robe, and nothing else, lay on her bed. She was dead.

She had been strangled. There were blue marks on her throat. Her face was hideous and her tongue protruded and looked black. Her fair hair was streaming on the pillow under her head and her ears were flat and ugly, with pointed tops and lobes.

So this was why she always wore her hair down. But what a thought, I later thought, to have at a time like that.

The room was in order. No picture was awry, revealing a safe from which Sally had taken the letters. The air-conditioning system which kept the house ventilated would probably have taken away the odor of the burnt letters by this time. Sally had probably burned them in her own room. She had a fireplace.

The men were examining the body. I slipped out and went to Sally's room. Strolled was the word, with Tisbury's snapping black eyes seeing everything.

There wasn't an ash in Sally's fireplace. No odor of burnt letters. So far, so good.

All at once Kim Forsythe muttered, "Don't let them come in here, Jean."

My heart moved into my throat, for a fact. "Where are you?"

"Under the bed."

"That's dumb!"

"You're telling me?"

"You ought to have your head examined, Kim. You'd better get out of here and come back in the front door."

"How?"

"Shush!"

Sally came in. She was crying.

"They think Kim did it. It seems Iles flew in about twenty minutes ago. They've got him at headquarters. Kim didn't come back with Iles. Iles swears he doesn't know where Kim is, says he walked out on him in Abilene. They thought at first he'd skipped for Mexico."

"Do you think Kim would do such a stunt?"

"No, I don't. What's more, they've traced him to Fort Worth. He took a plane to Forth Worth. They really think he's in Dallas. They think he did . . . that second awful thing. Oh, Jean!"

Sally was breaking up. That wouldn't do at this time.

"Look, Sally, Tisbury will have to telephone for his experts. Wangle him to the phone in the bar, won't you? I'll tell you why later on. I've got to fix my skirt and then I'll be right down."

"Why not tell me why now?"

"Do as I say, Sally."

To my surprise she didn't argue. She went out. In a moment I heard her and Patrick and Tisbury talking as they went downstairs.

I wondered how much Patrick knew. I knew darn well that Tisbury hadn't the faintest notion that Kim was in this house or he wouldn't have been led down like a lamb. He was about the least lamblike policeman I'd ever met.

"Come out of there, Kim!" Kim scrambled out. I wiped a smudge off his face and ran a comb through his hair, which being a crew cut stood right back up the way it was any way. I brushed off his clothes. "Now pussfoot down the back stairs, go through the kitchen and outdoors and come back in by the front door."

"Come back in?"

"Certainly. You've got to come in. You have to show."

"But what do I say?"

"Look, you've got to dream up your own answers. I'm just giving you a break. I don't know why exactly."

"I can explain . . ."

"There isn't time."

"But I didn't kill Rosemary. She was dead when I got here."

"Darling, I'd be screaming like mad if I thought you had. Go out and come in just as if you're just arriving. And put some zoom into it, Kim. Now, scoot."

I followed him into the hall and saw him disappear in the service stairs. I was shaking all over. I went back to pin up my skirt. I could hardly make a row of little gold pins look neat enough, considering all the time I had taken. I ran the same comb through my hair, put on some of Sally's lipstick, and then found a cigarette and lit it and hurried down the front stairs.

The others were all standing in the bar. Tisbury was cradling the phone when I got there.

"Mrs. Dollahan and Mr. Brady are at headquarters," he said. "They stopped in because of Mr. Dollahan. They're coming right out." He looked at me. "By the way, there was a mysterious call half an hour ago from a warehouse district. We sent out a prowl car and picked up a couple of men who had been tied up and left in a vacant house." His eyes snapped. "Our men found a lipstick in one of the rooms and outside in the alley was a message written with lipstick saying to call the police and call Patrick Abbott. The color matched the lipstick found in the house where the men were tied up."

"I'm afraid it won't be much use any more as a lipstick," I said.

Tisbury said, "Nylon stockings had been used to tie one man." Tisbury took in my bare ankles. "One of the men is dumb. The other tells a story which the dumb man says isn't so."

"How does a dumb man say something?" I inquired.

"He writes it," Tisbury said. "He insists they were attacked by burglars. He says there wasn't any woman there at all. But the one that talks say different. Okay, Mrs. Abbott. What cooks?"

The doorbell rang.

"I'll take that," Tisbury said. "I'll continue with you later, Mrs. Abbott."

Patrick's eyes were laughing.

"Why don't you say something, Pat?"

"Let him finish what he has to say first, Jean."

Because I had always gone into this room through the living room it was the first time I had noticed that there was a door directly into the main hall. It was quite near the front entrance. It fitted so neatly into the panelling that only the door-handle, the latch sort, was visible, and you wouldn't notice that unless you knew it was there. Tisbury left this door open and opened the front door.

Kim Forsythe walked in.

"Kim!" Sally cried, emotionally.

Kim wiggled a cheerful finger.

"Hi, everybody. Hello, Lieutenant. You still here?"

"Well, long time no see!" Tisbury said.

"How's that?"

"You'd better tell us where you've been," Tisbury said.

"Midland, Odessa. Back to Abilene. Flew from Abilene to Fort Worth, and got off then and took a bus."

"We knew you'd got to Fort Worth. Why didn't you fly on to Dallas?"

"Thoughtless of me," Kim said. "Do you know yet who killed Mrs. Juliana Willoz?"

"No mystery about that," Tisbury said. "You're not getting anywhere with the cute talk, Forsythe. How long have you been back in Dallas?"

"That I can't tell you to the minute, Lieutenant. I saw a taxi out on the highway, managed to signal it through the window, and the driver let me off the bus. I wanted to come here before coming to headquarters."

"Why?"

"That I can't tell you at the moment. What difference does it make?"

"Plenty. Of course you don't know that Rosemary Willoz is lying upstairs dead?" Kim gave a good imitation of astonishment. "Now, don't tell us you haven't any alibi again, Forsythe. The cab brought you right to the door, of course. A lot of people saw you. You'll know the exact time. The driver will back you up, too."

"As a matter of fact he probably won't," Kim said. "I didn't notice his name or number. I got out on Turtle Creek boulevard and crossed the creek on some driftwood. I did a little wading, too. Look!"

He'd done that all right, I thought. He'd even got his feet wet, and the bottoms of his trousers.

I was quivering all over. I was scared. I thought his answers were too slick. I wondered what I had got myself into, now. First, by being so obscure about those two men, in that old house, and now this tangle with Kim. Every word he was saying getting us both in deeper. They'd find a sunburned hair under that bed, sure as shooting. I wished I had had a chance to talk to Patrick before making myself Kim's accomplice.

Not that I wouldn't do it again. I knew he hadn't killed Rosemary, but his answers were much too smooth.

Tires sounded in the drive. I stepped near a window and saw Amanda parking her car near the garage.

A patrol car was stopping behind Tisbury's sedan, which was parked behind ours on the street.

Amanda, Iles and Lucius Brady came into the house. Amanda saw us from the hall. They all came into the bar.

Amanda's face was inscrutable. It said nothing. How much had Tisbury said before I came downstairs? When he telephoned for them to come home? Had she known we were here? Did she know about Rosemary? Was her self-control again functioning one hundred percent?

Iles showed his puzzlement. Brady was surprised and polite.

"Why the huddle?" Iles asked. Then he looked at Kim. "Say, what happened to you, son?"

"I ran out on you, Iles."

"How come?"

"You know that big ship which was warming up when you went to telephone? It was heading for Dallas. I left word for you with one of the mechanics."

"I reckon he didn't find me."

"I'm sorry, Iles. I had to get back, you see."

"He had to get back all right," Tisbury said. "He was in such a big hurry that he got off the plane at Forth Worth and took a bus. Leaves a fast plane for a slow bus, if you please. Mrs. Dollahan, there's no pleasant way to say what I have to say to you now. Your sister has been murdered."

"But I know that," Amanda said.

"I mean the other sister. Miss Rosemary."

Amanda did not breathe. She stood like a statue. She looked dead.

Then she reached out a hand, vaguely, and Iles stepped towards her and put an arm about her. Tisbury watched her without mercy. He watched us all. The black-widow eyes made a complete circuit. They seemed to ask, if it wasn't young Forsythe, who was it? One of you did it, the eyes said, and we aim to know which. *Sure enough!*

22

AMANDA whispered, "Where is she?"

Tisbury spoke gently. "Upstairs, ma'am."

"I must see her!"

"I wouldn't, ma'am." Iles asked then to see the body. "I'm sorry," Tisbury said. "You'd better wait till I've got some help."

Iles was indignant.

"Can't we even call our doctor?"

"Sure," Tisbury said. He waved at the phone. "But it's much too late for any doctor. He'd better not go in there either till the police get here. We don't want anything disturbed."

"Let me call him for you," Brady suggested, considerately.

He got the number and made the call. The rest of us sat down. Iles got Amanda a glass of brandy and asked if there was any objection to the rest of us having a drink. There was, Tisbury said. He advised sobriety. "Everybody better keep a clear head," he said.

Lucius Brady went over and talked softly to Amanda. He was offering sympathy. She gave him her hand, which he pressed beautifully, and after finishing with a word or two in the same vein to Iles and Sally he asked Tisbury if he might go.

"It's an appointment at my hotel. I'll come back at once, if you wish. Surely I can be of some use?" he said then to Iles.

"There ain't a thing you can do," Iles said gruffly. "I reckon the law will handle everything now."

Tisbury said there was no objection to Brady's going away provided he could be easily contacted. Something might come up. Brady said he would be constantly at his hotel and that he would return here within the hour. "Okay by me," Tisbury said.

Brady was actually going into the hall before Patrick said, "You know, Lieutenant, Mr. Brady may have been the last to see Miss Willoz alive."

Brady turned. He looked profoundly amazed.

"I say, Mr. Abbott?"

"Excepting the murderer, of course. You lunched with Miss Willoz, didn't you, Mr. Brady?"

"Why, yes. I did. But that's hours ago now."

Tisbury took over. "What happened then?"

Brady spread out the beautiful hands.

"Why, nothing at all. We lunched at Mario's and Miss Willoz dropped me at my hotel on her way home."

"What time was that?"

"I'm not sure exactly. Between two-thirty and three."

"You're sure she came home?"

"She expected to, Lieutenant. We used a taxi, and she instructed the driver to bring her here after dropping me downtown." The hands waved. "Of course, I don't know that she came home at that time. But she certainly expected to."

"She didn't say what her plans were?"

"No. Of course, with Mrs. Willoz . . ." He waved his hands, thus eloquently reminding us that Mrs. Willoz's funeral awaited, that that meant special preparations on the part of the family, and so on.

Amanda spoke up.

"I was at home when my sister arrived here. She came directly here after dropping Mr. Brady. She was alone. I left her here, alone."

Sirens announced the approach of the police cars. "Wait a few minutes, please, Mr. Brady," Tisbury said.

"Yes, of course. May I phone my hotel to leave a message about being delayed?"

"Sure."

The usual crew was arriving. Two men in uniform, a photographer, a fingerprint man and other experts. The Dollahans' doctor arrived too. Leaving Sergeant Gomez as our chaperone, Tisbury asked Iles Dollahan to go with him upstairs. Brady phoned his message and then lit a cigarette and sat down and talked to Amanda. Sally and Kim retreated to a corner and talked earnestly in whispers. Patrick smoked a cigarette and prowled around looking at the pictures of oil derricks and workers in overalls. I followed him. We singled out Iles Dollahan in the various pictures. His hair had silvered but he had not changed very much through the years. He was a wonderful-looking man always.

We could hear the police overhead, and on the stairs.

Iles came down. He looked gray with horror. Without asking permission this time he walked over and poured himself a stiff drink. He gulped it, and kept silent. Amanda watched him almost furtively.

Tisbury came back.

"Well, you've put a rope around your neck this time, Forsythe," he said grimly. Kim and Sally stood up, automatically, slowly. Both gaped as if stunned. "Your fingerprints are all over that room. Other evidence, too. So you were in this house before you presumably arrived after we did?"

Kim said, "Yes, I was."

"How did you manage it?"

"Just the way I said I did. Took a taxi and crossed the creek on the driftwood. Only, that time I didn't get my feet wet."

"In other words you lied?"

"Yes, sir."

"How did you get into the house?"

"The terrace door was not locked."

"Why did you kill her, Forsythe?"

"I didn't kill her."

"See here, people who lie about one thing will lie about another. You killed her."

Kim gave the detective his straight-forward honest gaze.

"I did not kill Rosemary Willoz. She was dead when I went into her room."

"Oh, you admit being in her room, do you?"

"Yes, I do. She had something which she refused to give back to me and I decided to get it, by any means. And when I got to her room she was . . . just the way she is now."

"Did you get what you came for?"

"No, I didn't."

"Because I got them first," Sally put in. "He's talking about some letters. I got them this afternoon before Rosemary came in. I burned them. They were in the wall safe in her room. It wasn't locked, and I found them and destroyed them."

"That implicates you, Miss," Tisbury said.

"Well, Kim didn't kill her," Sally said. "He was not in this house before he got here just now."

Their hands met and clasped.

"Yes, I was, Sally. I hid in your room."

"And it was my idea," I said, "for him to go out and come in again."

"For God's sake, Mrs. Abbott. You ought to know better than to do a thing like that!"

"I'm sorry. But he's telling the truth, so why shouldn't I? That boy did not kill anybody."

"In that case," Tisbury asked me sarcastically, "who did?"

Iles interrupted.

"They're right," he said. "The boy never did it. And I'll see that he gets the best counsel in Texas, Lieutenant. He don't have to talk now with that fellow over there writing everything down." Iles jerked his head at Sergeant Gomez, who went right on taking down his notes, just the same. "I don't blame my daughter and Kim for getting the letters. Rosemary was blackmailing Kim right along. She wanted him herself. I'd've got the letters too, come hell or high water, in their place."

"*With murder?*" Tisbury said.

"Aw, nuts!" Sally Dollahan said.

"Oh, please!" Amanda cried, and she began to cry. Iles went over to her. "I'm sorry to speak rough, Amanda. But the boy's life is at stake and he never did it, hear? It was somebody else, both times. It wasn't Kim."

"But my sister . . . my sisters . . . all my family. . . ."

Patrick said drily, "You've still got your brother, you know."

There was a crisp silence.

"The resemblance of your sister Rosemary and the dumb man who, shall we say, detained my wife in a house which belongs to you, Mrs. Dollahan, is pretty obvious. The eyes. The ears."

"Just what is this?" Iles bellowed.

Tisbury looked as if about to throw up the sponge. But Patrick went on.

"My wife was kidnapped this afternoon, Iles. By what seemed to be a couple of thugs. She was taken to a house in the warehouse district and detained there until, with your daughter's help, I found her. The house is your wife's property. The cab also."

"Is Ed back in this country, Amanda?"

Amanda nodded at her husband. "He said he was cured. He promised to lay off that awful stuff if I would help him. The cab was to be made over to him as soon as he could get a license."

"Did you have anything to do with what happened to Jean?"

Amanda nodded.

"I thought if we got her away Pat would stop prowling around this place. He was here this morning, poking around the premises. I knew Ed wouldn't hurt Jean, so I got hold of him, and then I called Lucius. I told him Jean was at Neiman's and for him to find her and stay with her a while. That I was having her followed and that way my detective, as I called Ed, would know who she was."

And Brady had pointed him out to me! Very fishy. My suspicion of Amanda was rising fast.

Tisbury said, "That is a pretty serious offense, Mrs. Dollahan."

"It is, if the Abbotts prefer charges," Iles said. He said it as if he hoped we wouldn't.

Patrick's eyes were green with anger and determination.

"Almost as serious as murder, Mrs. Dollahan," he said.

He was accusing her, I thought. I watched her. I saw her take hold of herself, put her chin up. I had to hand it to her.

"Patrick Abbott had no right to be hanging around this place. I wanted to get rid of him."

Tisbury said, "He was here with my permission, Mrs. Dollahan. He had a theory that Mrs. Willoz was shot from the opposite bank of the creek. It was pretty loopy. . . ."

"Not at all," Patrick said. "I've got the bullet."

"You what?"

"I've been too busy to report it, Lieutenant. It's in my bag, at the hotel. It was fired from the boulevard bank of the creek. The gun wasn't a forty-five. A thirty-two, I should judge. But I had to let the bullet wait until I collected my wife. Too bad, because in the meantime Rosemary Willoz was murdered. We might have saved her life if . . . if I hadn't had to consider Jean's safety just at the time I did."

Amanda burst into wild weeping. Iles comforted her but Patrick talked on, lifting his voice above her sobs.

"If. If. There are always these ifs. If I had not asked Jean to meet me in Dallas I would now be vacationing in New Mexico. If Jean hadn't got softhearted and fetched our dog with her the murder of Juliana Willoz would not have been discovered when it was and thus the murderer might have got away with it. If Rosemary Willoz hadn't had the kind of intuitive mind she had, so that she sensed who had done this murder, she might still be alive. Because her murderer is ruthless. Ambitious. Greedy. Ruthless. Your sister Juliana made a will, didn't she, Mrs. Dollahan? Leaving everything to Rosemary?"

Iles said, "I can answer that. Yes, she did. She hadn't a great deal, and Rosemary was not speaking the truth when she said she got a big settlement with the annulment of her marriage. She didn't get a cent. Amanda supported Rosemary. And when Juliana hadn't a great lot of money they decided among themselves that she had better leave what she did have, should she happen to die, to Rosemary."

"And Rosemary also made a will?"

"Yes, she did. So did Amanda. They got together and fixed up their business. At my suggestion, too."

"That's fine," Patrick said. "Now Mrs. Dollahan won't have to share Juliana's fortune with her brother Ed."

Amanda perked up.

"How dare you? Would I kill the one I love most in life except my own husband? For money? We already have all the money we'll ever need."

"Oil money comes and goes."

"Not Amanda's," Iles said. "She won't gamble like I do. I was mad at her last night because she wouldn't invest in the wildcat scheme which Kim and I flew out to cinch today. That's why Kim brought his gun. We didn't know what all we might run into out there. Maybe Amanda's right about my new deal." He grinned and said, "I always tell her she'll take care of me in my old age even though I don't hold with her buying so much jewelry from Brady."

"She's never made a bad buy, Iles," Brady said.

"This is getting off the beam," Tisbury said. "Pat, you'd better get that bullet. The rest of you stay here . . ."

Brady said, "If I might go also for a short time, Lieutenant? Perhaps the Abbotts will be so kind as to let me ride with them? I could come back within an hour, perhaps sooner."

"Go ahead," Tisbury said.

On the way downtown Brady apologized for the dinner which would not come off. It wasn't a good idea to start with, really, but of course he had ordered a private dining room, and all. His idea really was to get those poor people away from the tragic house, brighten them up a little. Now . . . well, it was all so dreadful! Poor Amanda. Poor, poor Amanda.

Nuts, I wanted to say, torn between the spectacle of Iles's proud loyalty to his wife, and her obvious cupidity. She was a ruthless, greedy, ambitious, wench in my opinion. Why hadn't Brady tumbled? And hadn't Tisbury guessed it all the time? But could they get her? What about Kim? Would they hold him on account of those fingerprints, even if they could pin the murder on Amanda?

We rolled up at the side entrance of Brady's hotel. He said he would see his client and try to join us outside the Adolphus within a few minutes. I was going to take this opportunity to change my clothes, so we said to make it roughly twenty minutes.

He left us and Patrick started the car.

At the corner he said, "Take over!" He slipped out on his side. I was stuck with the car. I drove it around to the hotel's main entrance and handed the keys to the doorman. I'd be back in a minute, I said, and I ran into the hotel just in time to see Patrick come from behind a pillar and go streaking up the stairs. I took the elevator. I remembered that Brady was on the third floor. I saw Patrick strolling along the hall as I got out of the elevator. I strolled after him and heard him knock on Brady's door.

"Maid, sir," he called, in a contralto I didn't know he possessed.

Brady opened the door and Patrick dived for him. "I figured he'd come after the gun," he said, as I entered. It was on the floor nearby. "Don't touch it, Jean."

"Even I know that much," I said, coldly.

"I wasn't sure," Patrick answered in the same tone.

23

"He confessed the whole thing," Tisbury said. "Good work, Abbott. Even though I am jealous."

Patrick grinned.

"Takes quite a cop to admit it, Lieutenant."

"I reckon I was dumb, sure enough."

"I had the great advantage of being on the spot," Patrick said. "And I had another advantage. You knew the guy by reputation. You took it for granted that he was okay because of his business standing and his friends. I'd never met him before, so I felt free to suspect him all along."

"Coca-cola, ginger ale, or soda?" a soft voice said. The colored waiter stood there smiling.

We were sitting at a table in the Century Room of the Adolphus, one of the tables up on a raised platform so you got a better view of the ice show. At the moment the dance floor was rolled out, instead of the rink, and people were dancing. We were not. The reason was under our table. Parked tight against my feet.

Lieutenant Tisbury had found us after we got here and had accepted our invitation to a drink and dinner.

It was after ten o'clock and he was off duty for the first time in more than twenty-four hours.

A pint of bourbon and another of scotch stood on the table, for this was Texas, and we were not in a private club. All the restaurant was allowed to serve was the mix. Texas is full of strange, strange contradictions.

"The confession covered practically everything," Tisbury said. "Well, you can't figure out a guy like that. He had a fine job, made loads of money, had a fine reputation. Been coming to Dallas for years and years. Always stayed at places like the Baker or the Adolphus or one of the hotels out near the Dallas Country Club. Everybody thought the world of him. Specially the women. Sort of a lounge lizard, but that goes with his trade, I reckon. And then all at once he goes loopy and kills two dames. Why?"

"He fell in love," I said.

"I don't think that's the whole answer, ma'am."

"He wouldn't've gone overboard except for the money, too," I said. "But he was nuts about Rosemary. I wasn't sure of it till today at lunch. I thought she was after Brady, too. But it was Kim Forsythe she really wanted. She told Brady so at lunch. She was doing all the talking and he simply lapped her up with his dreamy eyes, for of course he had left off his specs, because that would remind her of his age."

"She was a mighty pretty girl," Tisbury said.

"Depends on your taste," I said coldly. "As I understand from the confession, she went home after dropping Brady at his hotel. Amanda was there. Amanda went out—that was when she went to that house where they took me but before going out she phoned Brady. He knew from Amanda that Rosemary was taking a nap. He went back to the house. Took a cab there. So, of course, you would have found that out. Nobody answered his ring. He found the terrace door open, went in, went upstairs, woke Rosemary, pled with her. She accused him of being after Juliana's money and of killing Juliana. So he strangled her. He went out, walked along the creek, crossed the bridge and picked up a cab on the boulevard."

"Sure enough," Tisbury said. Meaning this time sure enough.

The waiter fetched the soda and a bowl of ice cubes and tongs. He took our dinner order. Patrick mixed the highballs. He said, "Brady was alone with Juliana Willoz a lot last night. She of course was very excited because she was coming into a fortune. She told him everything. He knew about the money and about her will. He agreed to go with her to Midland this morning. He lied to you about why he took her car, but of course she had asked for secrecy. He thought he would marry her. But he couldn't do it. Because he was crazy about

Rosemary. When he gave his supper party he absented himself for a few minutes. He had tipped a waiter to tell him he had a long distance call. We went to his room and got his revolver. He carried a gun in his bag, because he often traveled with a fortune in jewels. He knew about Juliana's quarrel with Amanda. She told him everything. It was true that Juliana slapped Amanda, not the other way around. She told him, as he confessed, that she was going back to see Amanda. She would walk. She preferred to. He took her car and he saw her open her door to leave the house. So he drove around the big irregular block and parked on the boulevard opposite a spot where she had to cross an open space. When she came in range he was hiding behind the car—that is, hiding from any possible spectators on the boulevard—and he shot her across the creek. The distance isn't more than thirty feet at that point. A gunshot would not be noticed on the boulevard. And with a gun the size of his it would not be heard from the house, with the creek and frogs and traffic all making noise. Then he jumped into the car and hared it for the hotel. It took him only five or six minutes extra time to wait and do the murder, and, as he said, he explained this small loss in time by saying he got lost. He didn't get lost. I figured he'd carry a gun and I wondered why you didn't look for it, Lieutenant."

"Because we never suspected him. We were all set to pin it on young Forsythe."

"I was betting on Amanda Dollahan," I said.

"She was number two with us, ma'am. And we thought her husband knew more than he let on, too."

"Iles was a mixture of mad and drunk," Patrick said. "He was mad at Amanda because she had bought those ruby clips but she wouldn't loosen up to go into his wildcat oil scheme. They had words, if I'm not mistaken, off and on all evening. But when Iles stepped out of the room he calls his bar and shot off that forty-five just for the hell of it, and under her window, she was frightened. She ran downstairs and out on the terrace. She dropped the red-horse clip. When he was all safe and sound she went upstairs again, madder than ever, of course. She missed the clip, and asked him to look for it. If he hadn't been a little tight he would have turned on the terrace lights to start with. His behavior all along during this time was that of a big direct-acting man who is mad and is drinking. He even came down to the hotel and threatened us with that gun because he thought we had the clip, which we had. By that time he was worried because he was afraid it would implicate Amanda."

"You should have given it to us," Tisbury said.

"I wanted Amanda to feel friendly towards us," Patrick said. "I couldn't figure her out."

"You could make her plenty of trouble for snatching you like that, Mrs. Abbott."

"Amanda's got enough trouble, Lieutenant."

Patrick nodded, and said, "Fortunately Pancho grabbed Iles in the leg and then Kim took over the gun, which is how you happened to find it on Kim. It was of course Kim's gun. They were armed for their little oil trip out in West Texas this morning."

There was wriggling in the neighborhood of my pumps and I said, "Be careful about that word P-a-n-c-h-o, Pat."

"I forgot. Well, Amanda was also frantic about the red horse because it was not yet insured. She is a very practical woman. But a loyal one, too. Her brother is a dope and has done time, as you know, but she stood by him. She would. Everybody has a weakness, and hers was Rosemary."

"Mighty pretty girl, sure enough," Tisbury said. "I sure hate to tangle with oil men. They don't know the meaning of the word law when they've got some deal on. Dollahan would have gone out West today no matter what, and he would have taken young Forsythe with him, too, so we figured the best thing was to give them the go-ahead and keep the Rangers on their tail out West. Which we did, but even so Forsythe gave us the slip. That boy's the real thing."

"How so?" I asked.

"Real oil man material, ma'am. I don't envy that girl Sally marrying that type, but I reckon she knows what she's up against. She's lived with it all her life."

"It's what she wants, Lieutenant. They'll be happy."

"Jean always knows," Patrick said. "She's never wrong on the love interest."

"I hope you're right, ma'am. But in the department we don't make such broad statements," Tisbury said. "This drink sure tastes good. First one I've had a chance to get outside of for some time. It's thanks to you, Abbott. If Brady hadn't confessed we'd've been on that case till kingdom come unless we got some other break."

"Too bad he won't hang," Patrick said.

"Yes, and no. Clears everything up to confess and saves the taxpayers money."

I asked, "Why did Brady call attention to the man following us from Neiman's? He knew that Amanda was back of that."

Patrick said, "He was getting ready to save his own face if Amanda got in too deep. He was getting ready to say that he thought he was being shadowed by the police and had told you so. The dumb man himself took a cab and went round the block to throw you off the track, Jean."

"That Rosemary!" I said. "I think she was mixed up somehow in Juliana's divorce. I'll bet that is why Juliana took the name Willoz again, because Rosemary was planning to become Mrs. Ulysses Green."

Tisbury's black eyes danced.

"You're right about that, ma'am. The police did get a little evidence, including that information. Seems Juliana didn't hold any grudge, though. Green himself changed his mind."

"Maybe he tumbled to what she was," I said.

"Mighty pretty girl, though," Tisbury said.

A champagne cork popped. Under the table Pancho emitted a discreet growl. I kicked him gently and smiled gaily at the police-detective. He was eyeing me hard.

"Don't growl like a d-o-g, Pat," I said, very gay.

Tisbury was not amused. "Are you breaking the law, ma'am?"

"Oh, Lieutenant Tisbury! He's such an angel. They'll never know he's here, if you don't give him away. He'll soon get used to champagne corks, because the smell of cordite doesn't come with the pops. It isn't as if we haven't done this before, you know."

Patrick said, "If it hadn't been for his giving us an early start on this case you wouldn't be free to have a drink with us now, Lieutenant."

I said, "We were famished. We'd got him from the kennel to take him to Sally Dollahan to keep for us till I did some shopping. Thanks to this murder case I haven't one thing left to wear. Well, Sally isn't home yet. so I kept you-know-who under my coat and here we all are."

"You haven't answered my question exactly," Tisbury said.

"Dallas is such a wonderful place to shop."

"Ma'am?"

The dog was stiff with worry. I could sense this, from the stiff way he sat against my ankles.

Patrick said, "What burns me is that P-a-n-c-h-o isn't any detective at all. He follows red herrings. Red horses, in this case. He's never uttered one bark against Brady. I'm positive now that that d-o-g is not such a g-o-d as he seems to think. Why, even if he could talk. . . ."

"He's perfect," I said. "Just perfect."

Tisbury sighed. "You're a slippery one yourself, Abbott. You lied about having found the bullet from Brady's gun."

"Right. But if I hadn't, Brady wouldn't've dashed right off to get rid of the gun. So here we are, everything fine, everything settled."

"Except who killed Sally's Sam," I said.

"The death of Sam will probably remain an unsolved mystery," Patrick said. "How about a dividend, Lieutenant?"

Tisbury thought it over very, very briefly. Then his teeth flashed in his charming smile and he pushed over his glass.

"I ought to have the law on you both," he said. Under the table Pancho relaxed. Everything was okay.

www.ingramcontent.com/pod-product-compliance
Lightning Source LLC
LaVergne TN
LVHW022138271025
824443LV00038B/1227